I0749369

The Reluctant Viscount

A Novel of Regency Romance

Teresa Sweeney

Courting Romance Publishing
California

Published in the United States by Courting Romance Publishing

ISBN 978-1-940319-03-2

First Edition

Cover Photography by Christina Brusaca
Cover Model: Lawrence Sweeney III

By Teresa Sweeney

Always Rebecca

A Love Match, Indeed!

An Uncommon Affair

The Reluctant Viscount

To my most outstanding son, Lawrence III.
Charming, clever, fearless.
I am so very proud of you.

The Reluctant Viscount

Chapter One

The Countess of Westfield rushed into her breakfast parlour to search for her brother William. Lady Elinor Westfield was put out of sorts to see he was not at the side table filling his plate with the hearty meal he took each morning. She could usually find him holding one of the many silver dome covers keeping the trays of food warm on the marble countertop, seeking out the hidden delicacies that made up the morning meal. It was easy to envision his cheeky smile at being caught tasting a morsel from his plate, before seating himself at the table to dine like a proper gentleman. She asked the attending footman if her brother had broken his fast and immediately grew concerned when he replied, "No, my lady."

Elinor's heart began to beat rapidly. She had not seen William nor received word from him since yesterday morning and she feared he had come to harm. Her brother was all but eight and ten, recently graduated from Cambridge and until of late, a young man of sense and consideration. It was unlike him not to leave word of his whereabouts.

London was full of villains, lurking in dark corners, just waiting to attack and rob those they considered weak and vulnerable. William was far from weak, but he did own an adventurous spirit that oftentimes placed him in dangerous situations. She shivered, remembering how frantic she became when she learned he had attended a bearbaiting rout and cockfight. The recollection led her to imagine all sort of grisly scenes where her brother lay mortally wounded in a dark alley and she immediately chastised herself for indulging his every whim. When William asked if he could come to London to spend time with her before he began his Grand Tour, she welcomed the idea. He would be gone two years, perhaps more, visiting museums and other historical, architectural, and religious sites of importance to round out his education. The Grand Tour was the rite of passage for all young men of the aristocracy. Accompanied by their tutor, they were expected to enrich their knowledge and also polish their social skills by attending the galas hosted by the elite society of the country they were touring. Now, Elinor worried her gullibility in believing she could protect her brother from London's temptations and seedy side had placed him at risk. She should have known his handsome face, trim physique, and amiable personality would draw others to include him in their jaunts. He was the image of their mother during her debut, whose raven black hair and sapphire-blue eyes had marked her a *diamond of the first water;* and also like her, William was well-liked and sought-after by his peers.

Elinor hurried to her husband's study and paused only a moment in front of the massive closed mahogany doors before she knocked abruptly. She knew her husband, Jonathan, the Earl of Westfield, was in conference regarding parliamentary issues. A number of bills were being discussed in the House of Lords and Lord Westfield, an attentive and responsible peer, had scheduled appointments to meet individually with some key noblemen to discuss his concerns. She hoped, as she pushed through the heavy doors, her gauche interruption would not cause any damage to her husband's efforts.

Jonathan saw his wife's distress the minute she entered his study and instinctively pushed his carved walnut wingback chair from his desk to stand, "What is wrong, Elinor?"

She did not bother to check her frantic behavior, greet her husband's guest, nor worry if her outburst might be tomorrow's parlour *on dit*. All she cared about was finding her brother, "William did not come home, Jonathan. I am besides myself with worry."

The earl walked around the desk to comfort his countess. He took her clammy hands into his own and squeezed them, stroking his thumbs across the backs of her hands while he looked into her hazel eyes. He tried to soothe her fears by offering an explanation, "William is only trying out his wings, Elinor. He is no fool and quite capable of taking care of himself. You must not aggrieve yourself so, especially in your condition."

Jonathan's words catapulted Elinor out of her trepidation when she remembered they were not alone. Her eyes widened in alarm and Jonathan, realizing his blunder, laughed. He turned to Edward Brentwood, the Earl of Felton, with whom he had been in conference, "I fear I have let out our little secret, Felton. Before long we will increase our family, giving your godson either a brother or sister to command."

Edward had risen the moment Elinor entered the study. An intimate of the Earl and Countess of Westfield, he had not excused himself as he ought in such a private moment, for he hoped he could be of service to his friends. Upon Jonathan's revelation, he advanced toward the happy couple and offered his congratulations, "This is wonderful news! Please, do not fret, Elinor. I will keep your secret until which time you make your formal announcement, though I do hope you give me leave to share the news with my wife. Anne has a profound acuity to know when I am withholding anything from her."

"Of course, Edward."

"I will have her call upon you, for I am sure she will wish to share our own good news with you."

Elinor forgot her concerns for William and embraced her good friend with alacrity. Jokingly, Jonathan scolded his emotionally excited wife, "Elinor, I fear you are damaging Felton's cravat. His fastidious valet, Jenkins, will never forgive you, should someone remark upon it."

"Oh, fustian! Edward and Anne are too dear to me to act with decorum. Besides, you will not abuse me in my fragile condition."

"You have never been fragile," chuckled Jonathan. "If anything, you are more robust when you are increasing."

Elinor's smile faded when she remembered why she had burst into the study to seek her husband. She was overwrought with concern, "What are we to do about William?"

"He accompanied Atwood to the Deneham's Rout. Did he not?"

"Yes."

Edward hated to see Elinor distressed and offered, "Atwood is my houseguest. Allow me to interview him on your behalf."

"You are too good, Edward. You will send word as soon as possible."

"Of course, Elinor. Do not be afeard. I agree with Westfield, William is just taking in too much amusement." Edward then said to Jonathan, "We will continue our discussion on the morrow, Westfield?"

"Thank you, Felton, that would be most agreeable."

Edward entered his posh Mayfair town home and handed his beaver hat, gloves, and greatcoat to his attending footman. He no sooner relieved himself of his outerwear when he heard female voices coming from the parlour alerting him his wife had company. His butler, Simmons, hurried towards him and the moment he made his greeting, Edward asked, “Who is here?”

“Lady Deneham and her daughter, Miss Margaret Deneham, my lord.”

Anxious to relieve Elinor of her worry, he inquired to see if his houseguest, Lawrence Cowper, Viscount Atwood, was at home. He was happy to learn he was present and keeping his wife and the Denehams company. Edward made his way to his parlour and balked when he spied Lawrence looking out of place in the gaggle of female conversation. The discomfited viscount made Edward want to chuckle. He would have enjoyed the comedic scene a bit more before presenting himself, except his entrance drew everyone's attention. It heartened him to note his wife's joy at seeing him. Her smile beckoned him and he hastened to greet her. He noticed Lady Deneham's grin of approval when he took his wife’s hand and raised it to his lips for a kiss.

“My lord husband!" exclaimed his wife cheerfully. "How good of you to join us. You are acquainted with Lady Deneham, but I do not know if you have met her daughter. Allow me to present Miss Margaret Deneham to you. Miss Deneham, my husband, Edward Brentwood, the Earl of Felton.”

Meg made her curtsey and extolled, “It is an honor, my lord.”

Edward smiled at the strikingly pretty dark-haired debutante with chestnut-brown eyes, "No, my dear. I assure you, the honor is mine." He then looked to Lady Deneham and Viscount Atwood, casting a nod in greeting, "What news do you bring, Lady Deneham?"

She replied with a chuckle, "Only news of a successful crush, my lord. I fear you have caught me in leave, so I will let her ladyship share the *on dits* of the evening as I trespass on her time no longer." She looked to her daughter, "Make your curtsey, Meg. We have stayed longer than propriety governs."

It looked as if Meg was about to burst out with giggles, but she refrained and with eyes gleaming, she gave a proper curtsey and bid her farewell. Edward caught Lawrence's scowl and wondered what caused his ill humor. His wife's inquiry about the well-being of the Westfields broke his reverie and he recalled his task at hand.

"Atwood, if you please, I would have a word with you."

"Of course, Felton. I am at your service."

Anne could tell her husband had pressing business with Lawrence and excused herself, explaining she was retiring to her room and would see them both later. Edward watched his wife depart, feeling a pang of regret for her abrupt exit.

"Is something amiss?"

Lawrence's query recalled Edward's attention and he turned to ask him, "By chance, do you know the location of young William? Lady Westfield is beside herself with worry. He has not returned home."

"I can only guess, Felton. William accompanied me to the Deneham Rout, but took his leave with some young rogues, friends from school I believe, for he seemed quite familiar with them. I expect he visited the clubs with them and is probably sleeping away the day at one of their apartments."

"I am sorry you could not dissuade him, Atwood. He is too inexperienced to run around London unguided, especially in such risky company."

"I am sorry, Felton. I fear I let Miss Deneham discommode me to distraction and when I looked to find William, I realized he had taken his leave."

Lawrence did not know what it was about Miss Deneham that always seemed to tie his stomach up in knots. He first met the young lady two years ago when the Marquis of Beaumont, Lord Felton's great-uncle, hosted a ball to honor Felton's betrothal to Lady Anne. Lawrence, newly titled, had been overwhelmed by the effervescent *marriage mart mamas* tickled pink to introduce their single daughters to him. They saw the unpolished young man as an easy prize to win and pushed their daughters to secure him. Lawrence was ill-prepared to manage the flaunting and obsequious debutantes accosting him with frivolous discourse and silk fans. He felt like a cornered animal and soon wearied of being attacked. He began to take refuge in the ballroom shadows, preferring to observe society from the corners of the room rather than being its focal point. He was discreetly watching the couples take their positions on the dance floor, when Miss Deneham caught his eye. She was remarkably pretty wearing a white lace skirt over a white satin slip, trimmed with Belgian lace and sea green ribbon. The high-waist gown with short puffy sleeves displayed her trim and shapely figure, plus the green trim complimented her chocolate-brown hair, luminous amber eyes, and fair skin. Lawrence was fascinated with her assured demeanor, sparkling eyes, and laughter. She seemed real compared to the other debutantes who acted as though they had never received a gentleman's attention before. He thought Miss Deneham revealed her true self and was a person of good humor, not someone performing to allure attention. It was her *joie de vivre* and beauty that beckoned admirers much like a mythical Siren lured sailors. He doubted she was dangerous, at least until he saw her hands lash out in enthusiasm while she chatted. He had to hold back a chuckle when her conversation peaked in excitement and she almost swatted a neighbor with the back of her hand. He could not take his eyes off her and his curiosity got the better of him. Without thought, he walked across the dance floor and found himself near enough to draw her attention. He was mortified when he realized he looked like he was attempting to introduce himself. He knew a respectable gentleman would look for a mutual acquaintance to make his introduction, anything less would be considered gauche by Society's rules. His embarrassment grew when she turned her attention from her friend and asked him, "I beg your pardon, but I do not believe we have been introduced."

Lawrence's mouth was too dry to speak. Before he had a chance to swallow and assert himself, Miss Deneham remarked, "Come now, I won't bite you. Tell me your name and I shall confess my own."

Her companion laughed and Lawrence turned and walked away.

Miss Deneham was sorry to see the handsome young man leave her company. She was thrilled when she saw him approach and wanted to appear witty and charming to impress him. Her companion identified him as Viscount Atwood and she found herself immediately attracted to him. It surprised her that her quip affronted him instead of engaging him in some light banter. Had she not just read in her *Minerva Press Novel* that Lady Josephine used the same remark to entice a prince?

Later that evening, the marquis formally introduced the cautious pair, but the damage was already done. The cheerful nature Lawrence had found so attractive, now peaked his anger. His temper spiked each time he saw Miss Deneham grin, for she looked as if she was laughing at him and he despised being the jest of a joke.

Soon after that fateful meeting, the marquis spirited Lawrence away on a tour of the Mediterranean countries to outwit those scheming mothers who plotted some kind of impropriety to force Lawrence's hand into matrimony. Beaumont hoped to build the young man's confidence and garner him the experience he needed to engage in the superior society of the *ton*. He also wanted to protect him from those conniving women who would use seduction to capture a naïve lord.

The tour served its purpose and Lawrence returned to London an experienced man of the world, a man not easily cajoled. He learned to hide his emotions and how to display an unaffected manner when confronted with barbs or schemes, except it seemed when in the company of Miss Deneham, whose simple smile irked him beyond reason.

Lawrence was still in retrospection when Edward asked, "You have no names for me to follow up? I would like to find the young cub and ease Elinor's mind."

"Allow me, Felton. It will appease my guilt to search William out for the Westfields."

"Very well, but be sure and keep me informed."

Chapter Two

Lawrence left Lord Felton's town home immediately after assuring his lordship he would keep him apprised of his search for William. He ordered Simmons to call to the mews for his carriage and the moment he spied his vehicle, he rushed down the front steps to jump into it, not waiting for his footman to lower the carriage step. He undoubtedly vexed his servant who took pride in his duties, but he was still adjusting to the pomp and circumstances of his title and wealth. At the moment he was in too much of a hurry to find William to adhere to protocol.

The elegant vehicle was the first extravagant purchase, aside from his clothes and horseflesh he made when he came into his title. Along with his land came substantial wealth, accumulated over the years from the rents paid by his once neglected tenants and other investments made by his predecessor. Lord Felton had counseled him to purchase the four-wheeled hardtop vehicle as evidence of his rank. The closed body carriage seated four comfortably and hung center over its suspension. There was an outside driving seat for his coachman and rumble seat in the back for a footman or two. His coat of arms were emblazoned on the highly polished doors to flaunt his peerage and wealth. The inside of the coach was embellished with velveteen squabs, silk linings, leather trims, drop down windows and secret compartments where items like liquor were stored to provide him every comfort. Under the seats were places for lap blankets and picnic baskets. There was even a vase screwed into the side paneling should the owner wish the adornment of a flower.

Lawrence shouted for his coachman to take him to St. James Street where he would learn if William had tried his hand at one of White's gaming tables. Both he and William were recently inducted into the private gentlemen's club. William's grandfather, the Duke of Hartford, had written the boy's name at birth into the club's candidacy book. When William made his majority, there was little concern he would be voted into the club's membership. No one with any sense would affront a family as titled or connected as William's. Lawrence, on the other hand, had to rely on the sponsorship of Lords Beaumont, Felton, and Westfield to speak on his behalf. He remembered being heavily concerned his common upbringing would prejudice the members against accepting him. His father was a merchant marine and regardless of his newly acquired peerage, he was sure the members would blackball him. The aristocrats were a fickle group. He heard of one nobleman who was rejected because his boots were not shined properly. It only takes one member to drop a black marble into the ballot box for a candidate to be denied membership.

Lawrence was nine and ten years old, alone in the world, before he learned he was the rightful heir to the Atwood title. The viscountcy laid in abeyance awaiting a male heir bearing the family mark of nobility. Lawrence's grandmother was the daughter of Viscount Atwood. Among her siblings, only her daughter produced a son with a crescent-shaped birthmark on his neck. His grandmother always said it was a mark of nobility, but until he met his great-aunt, Baroness Litford, who validated his claim, Lawrence had never believed her.

He thought himself without family after his mother died. During his lifetime, the only male name he ever heard mentioned with affection was the Marquis of Beaumont. His grandmother had spoken of him kindly and since he knew nothing of his grandfather, other than he died in service for his country, he began to wonder if the marquis was his mother's natural father. Finding himself without money or connections to make his way in the world, he sought out the nobleman. It was through the Marquis of Beaumont's and Lord Felton's assistance he discovered his great-aunt lived, and through her, he learned he was the rightful heir to the Atwood title. Baroness Litford authenticated his claim and the Prince Regent signed the letters patent bestowing his title and properties upon him.

Lawrence was not totally surprised William and his friends were not at White's. He had thought the young lord might have wanted to impress his friends with his exclusive membership, but he also knew the conventional gentleman's club was probably too dull for the rowdy evening they planned. He headed to Crockford's, hoping their pursuits did not take them into the gaming hells, where a young man could be introduced to more than gambling.

He entered the up-and-coming fashionable club and was not surprised to see, even at this early hour, a few players at the green baize tables. His eyes scanned the room and a gentleman sitting alone, shuffling a deck of cards, caught his attention. The man looked up, "Looking for Crawford?"

It took a minute for Lawrence to realize William, the son of the Earl of Ingall, was indeed Lord Crawford, Viscount Crawford. It was a common practice for the peerage to distinguish their younger sons in Society by giving them one of their inferior titles. He realized he and William held the same rank, except William was in line to an earldom and a dukedom, once his father and grandfather passed. It was no wonder Lady Westfield feared for his safety. His connections and prospects exposed him to the devious-minded scoundrels who were constantly on the lookout for an inexperienced and young lord. Many of whom, once reaching their majority, are anxious to come to London to experience those attractions learned of by older brothers and acquaintances. It was not uncommon for these young bucks to fall into the hands of card sharks who were famous for letting them win before having their luck turn on them. In their earnestness, to recapture their losses, they would risk even more. Scandals of properties and/or fortunes lost at the tables were common *on dits* among the *ton*.

Lawrence would always be thankful Beaumont and Felton had the foresight to help him gain the polish he needed to protect himself from the unscrupulous. While his grandmother and mother tutored him in the academic fields and raised him to the manners of a gentleman, he was still ill-equipped when he first joined the aristocracy to deal with the duplicitous nature of those wishing to take advantage of him. He understood his position and wealth made him a target for the *marriage mart mamas* and deceitful men. His time abroad taught him to be cautious and to consider the motive of someone wanting to be acquainted with him, so he naturally suspected the gentleman who pointed out William's location.

Lawrence strode to where William slouched sound asleep in a high-backed red velveteen wingback chair. His cravat was loosened and his hair mussed from what appeared to be a long and hard night's rest. Lawrence kicked at William's outstretched legs, jostling him to alertness. William's heavy eyelids sluggardly opened and he pulled himself up to a proper sit. With his sonorous voice, he cursed, "I beg your pardon!" However, when he recognized Viscount Atwood as the intruder to his slumber, he exclaimed, "Atwood! I am so glad to see you. Perhaps, now I will get some satisfaction."

William's words alarmed Lawrence who feared the young man had embroiled himself in a duel. There were still too many young lords who romanticized the swordfight or the use of pistols at dawn to settle a dispute. Challenges were issued in earnest, even though these contests were frowned upon by society. Lawrence checked his concern and ignored William's remark, "Your sister is overwrought with your tardiness, Crawford. I suggest we make our way to her, so you can make your apologies."

William rose and explained with fervor, "You do not understand, Atwood. I am honor-bound to stay. The chap won't except my *vowels* nor will he produce his direction, so I may call on him to settle my account."

Lawrence glanced over to the blond-haired man who lacked the dress of a gentleman, his unfashionable brown worsted coat hung loosely on him and he bore no cravat. His sun-tanned skin gave him a rustic look, but his straight posture, perceptive eyes, and confidence marked him a man of distinction. Lawrence guessed his age to be around six and twenty and began to take the man's measure until he saw the man's mouth turn up in a grin. The stranger stood and proudly gave his name, "Kevin Donahue."

Lawrence noted the accent and realized the man was American. He thought Mr. Donahue was about to offer him his hand in greeting until he heard his curt introduction, "Lawrence Cowper, Viscount Atwood. May I ask what business you have with his lordship that keeps him from his family?"

Kevin smirked, "The boy's stubbornness keeps him here because I refused his IOUs, not me. I should have refused to play with him, but it was obvious he was in his cups, and I thought I was doing him a favor, keeping him away from the card sharks." Grinning, he added, "He is quite the chatterbox when he has imbibed and kept me fully entertained. I played with him to amuse myself, not to take advantage of him. He insists I take his *vowels*, but I am sure he does not have the funds and I will not have it on my conscious he applied to a money lender. Believe me, no one knows of his foolishness, aside from us. I made it look as though he paid his debt, but if we continue with this discourse, I am sure word will spread soon enough. I suggest you take the young man home and educate him on when to bluff, before he tries his hand at cards again." Mr. Donahue picked up and pocketed the coins that were left on the green baize card table and started to leave.

William demanded, "You must get his direction, Atwood! I must be allowed to settle my debts. You know my honor is at stake!"

Lawrence stepped in front of Mr. Donahue, "Crawford is right, Mr. Donahue. We British are single-minded when it comes to *debts of honor*."

"Very well. I am staying at the George Inn. You may settle his accounts with me there."

A very relieved Lady Westfield embraced her brother when Lawrence brought the young man to the Westfield town home. Elinor knew better than to question her wearied sibling, who looked like he was sleepwalking. Instead, she suggested he retire to his room where he could have a hot bath, repose, and then partake on the platter of food she would order Cook to send up to him. His stomach was growling something fierce and Elinor felt a pang of sympathy for her exhausted and hungry brother. William soberly nodded that he would do as she bid.

Then, the countess requested Lawrence join her in her day parlour. They entered in tandem. Elinor made her way to the bell cord and gave it a tug before returning her focus to Lawrence who remained near the threshold, "You must be famished, my lord. Please take a seat. I will order us a repast and ask my lord husband to join us."

When her butler arrived, she instructed him to inform the earl Viscount Atwood had called and commanded him to have Cook send a tray of food to her brother and a tea tray with some sandwiches for her and her guest. Not a moment passed before Lord Westfield entered the room. It seemed he was making his way to see Elinor before he was even informed about his visitor. He was happy to hear William returned home unscathed; though his smile flattened when he saw Lawrence's concerned face, "Well, let's have the worst of it. How much has he lost?"

Elinor's eyes widened, "Lost what, Jonathan?"

She scanned across her husband's face to Lawrence's reserved countenance. When realization came, she exhaled a simple, "Ahh!"

It was at this moment the butler announced the arrival of the Earl and Countess of Felton and asked if they were at home to receive them. Lawrence explained, "I sent him a note the minute I found William. He must be here to learn of his welfare."

Jonathan ordered his butler to present them while Elinor told him to bring more food to accommodate her arriving guests. The butler nodded in obedience and returned with Lord and Lady Felton. No sooner were the greetings made when Elinor proposed to Anne they leave William's folly in the gentlemen's hands and visit her son Stephen. She suggested to her friend and son's godmother they retreat to the nursery for their own *tête-á-tête* where they could share with each other their own good news. Anne cheerfully agreed and both women departed, arm in arm, knowing they would be apprised later of what was discussed.

"Well go on," demanded Jonathan. "How much did William lose?"

"One hundred fifty pounds," replied Lawrence. "The gentleman is American. He was not interested in taking William's *vowels,* nor would he give him his direction. That is the reason why William would not return home last night. He felt honor-bound to repay the gentleman."

Edward laughed while Jonathan asked, “There is more?”

“The American claims he was being kind having recognized that William was an inexperienced card player. He says he played with him to keep away those who were ready to take advantage of him by raising the stakes and would not be responsible for William seeking out a moneylender to settle his debt, since he feared he did not own the fund’s himself.”

“That is indeed true,” said Jonathan. “But surely he knows his connections, his family’s wealth.”

“I doubt it. His dress suggested he recently arrived in London, for I cannot imagine any other reason for him to stand out in our elevated Society in such unfashionable garb.”

“He might not care, Atwood," remarked Edward. "These Americans are not as fastidious in their attire as we British.”

“You have his direction, Atwood?” asked Jonathan.

“Indeed, he is at the George Inn. Will you apply to his father?”

“Nay, William leaves on his Grand Tour in two days. I won’t upset Elinor’s parents before his departure. Let the Ingalls enjoy the ignorance of his reckless behavior.”

Lawrence laughed, remembering the American's comment, “The American suggested we tutor William on when to bluff. It seems he is wanting in that area.”

“You liked him, Atwood?” inquired Edward.

“He gave a good impression, not arrogant, but confident. He is a man who knows who he is and has no issues with it."

“I would like to meet him."

“I, as well,” added Jonathan. “It is proper I thank him in person. I will send him a voucher to repay William’s debt with an invitation to join us at White's for tomorrow. What say you, Felton? Will you come?”

“I will make myself available.”

“I would like to attend also,” asserted Lawrence. “If it is agreeable to you both.”

“Of course,” replied Jonathan. “All we need to know is the gentleman’s name.”

“Kevin Donahue."

Mr. Donahue paid his fare to the hackney driver and took a moment to look up at the private and esteemed gentleman's club with its unique bay window. The white building was three stories tall with a Palladian facade that boasted eight grand columns with five tall windows, one window placed between each set of pillars. The central window was arched, while the other four windows were corniced with French motif decorations above them. Ever since the Italian architect Andrea Palladio revived the classical style in the 1550's, the Roman/Greek architecture has been prevalent in England and Scotland among the aristocracy.

Kevin shrugged off his admiration of the building and raced up the steps to enter the exclusive club. He was greeted by its formidable majordomo and unconsciously held his breath waiting to see if he would be allowed entry. He exhaled in relief when he learned his name was prominently placed on the guest list by the Earl of Westfield. The austere butler led him into the drinking parlour. Kevin followed the stiff-backed butler to a table where three gentlemen and the young Lord Crawford sat. It pleased him to see their mouths momentarily gape open. It was clear to him they were all surprised to see him eloquently dressed wearing a blue form-fitting superfine double-breasted coat and tan-colored breeches that hugged his athletic legs. His cravat was tied in a simple knot, bearing no jewel or stickpin and even though his boots were only adequately polished, missing the sheen valets achieved with the use of a champagne polish, his bold stride and confident air drew attention to him. It would be hard-pressed to class him as anything, but a gentleman in Society. Aside from his bronzed skin, the rural look Lawrence had remarked about him at first acquaintance was gone.

Upon his arrival into fashionable London, Kevin was immediately made aware, while walking along the store fronts of Bond Street and Picadilly, that his attire marked him an inferior gentleman. The discriminating looks he received bothered him. He was a man used to working with his hands and had never paid much attention to his clothes, other than they were clean and in good repair until he landed in England. His good looks had always been enough to win any young lady's admiration, but he learned quickly, when his greetings were rebuffed, that English women judged a man's character by his clothes. Apparently, a *gentleman* was a man who did not engage in labor, but was a man with property and enough capital to live leisurely and dress immaculately. While Kevin did not live an idle life, he had no intention of being judged poorly because of his attire. He immediately found a tailor and commissioned himself a wardrobe.

He was happy when one of the new suits he ordered arrived in time for his meeting with the lords. Kevin had not been ignorant of Atwood's appraisal of him the day they met. He wanted the opportunity to change the man's opinion, so it pleased him when his lordship smiled with approval.

Jonathan was the first to rise and greet Kevin. William quickly performed the formal introductions and after everyone made their salutation, Lord Westfield asked Mr. Donahue to take a seat. He ordered a round of drinks for his party and then thanked Mr. Donahue for his kindness to William, who was quick to add his own gratitude, "I am forever in your debt, Mr. Donahue. I realize I would be in dire circumstances had I played with anyone else. I am leaving on my Grand Tour, but I hope you will feel free to call on me should I ever be of service to you." William presented him with his card and proffered his hand earnestly.

Kevin took and pocketed William's card before shaking his hand, "Your gratitude is unnecessary, my lord. You were good company and I assure you, that I was only extending the same kindness shown to me in my *salad days* (youth). I only hope that one day you will remember to repay in kind."

Lords Westfield and Felton looked at each other with surprise. Edward was the first to speak, "That is most magnanimous of you, Mr. Donahue. I commend your philosophy, but warn you there are those in our Society who would easily take advantage of it and never once reciprocate."

Kevin laughed, "I assure you, I am not naïve, my lord. Let us say, I recognized William's initiation into gambling and chose to take him under my wing. I do not make a habit of refusing to take my lawful winnings." A thought came upon him and he shared his revelation, "As it is, I have my prize in making the acquaintance of honorable men. I dare say, my philosophy, has multiplied my wealth."

William raised his glass and toasted, "Here! Here!"

Jonathan smiled at his brother-in-law's youthful display and raised his glass with everyone else. He liked the American and his curiosity of him prompted him to learn more about him, "What brings you to England, Mr. Donahue? Do you have family here?"

"I am hoping it is my accent and not my clothes that gives evidence of my American background, for the tailor I commissioned for a new wardrobe assured me I would be in the *pink of fashion*."

"I must beg your pardon for my scrutiny of you upon our first introduction, Mr. Donahue," apologized Lawrence with a grin. "I will be the first to commend your wardrobe. You are indeed fashionable and will pass muster with our *bon ton*. However, we must get Felton's valet, Jenkins, to polish your boots."

"As long as their lack of shine is not a hanging offense," chuckled Kevin in reply. "I would not impose on his lordship's valet."

"Who says it is not?" retorted Edward.

Kevin smiled, enjoying the gentleman's wit, before remembering to answer Lord Westfield's question, "I am here on family business. I do not know if I have any relatives here, even though my great-grandmother originally hailed from England."

"May I inquire on the nature of your family's business, Mr. Donahue?" asked Edward.

"We grow and export tobacco. We have an agent we use to make these trips for us; however, I came in his stead and was commissioned to complete some other acquisitions for my family and neighbors. My sister is betrothed and my mother wants me to buy some wedding gifts. My neighbors learned of my trip and added to my purchases."

William asked, "Would it not have been easier to buy your items in America?"

Kevin shrugged his shoulders, "Easier, yes, but the items requested are imported from England. In America, selection is almost nonexistent. The prices for these products are ridiculously high considering their quality. I had volunteered to make the trip for our agent since his wife recently presented him with a son. It seemed reasonable to task me with making the additional purchases and ensure their safe delivery."

"What sorts of items do you wish to purchase?" inquired Edward.

"Furniture, porcelain, drapery and other odds and ends."

"I have a very capable man of business who is remarkable in accomplishing the most miniscule of tasks," offered Edward. "I would consider it my pleasure if you would allow him to locate these items for you. Be assured, you would inspect them before purchase to ensure they meet your requirements."

"You are too kind, my lord, but it is unnecessary."

"I beg to differ, Mr. Donahue, I am a businessman and your venture intrigues me. I see an opportunity to expand my export trade. I am interested in talking to you in depth regarding where you live and what is available in your territory."

Jonathan laughed, "I should have known you would find a way to increase your coffers, Felton." Jonathan thought Elinor would like to meet the pleasant man who helped her brother and extended the American an invitation to dine, "I hope you will come to dinner tomorrow, Mr. Donahue, and meet my wife. Felton you will bring Anne and Atwood." Looking at Kevin he asked again, "You will come?"

“I would be honored.”

“The Denehams are expected tomorrow, Westfield. Allow me to act as host," suggested Edward. "Elinor will not be too inconvenienced to come to my home?”

“She would not miss it. Until tomorrow.”

“I will send my coach to pick you up, Mr. Donahue," concluded Edward. "Shall we say eight o’clock?”

“I will be ready. Thank you.”

Chapter Three

Miss Margaret Deneham followed her parents up the steps to the Earl of Felton's affluent town home, smiling at her parent's affectionate manner. It was a common occurrence to see them huddle together like conspirators, her mother whispering in her father's ear and him, chuckling in response. She watched her father take her mother's elbow to help her through the front door. She stored the image as another example to combat the ancient rumor her parents *married for convenience*. Meg was aware members of the *ton* still believed her parent's marriage was far from a *love match*. It was the only explanation the *gossipmongers* were comfortable with in understanding why a devilishly handsome man married a lady beneath him in looks and grace.

Sir Marcus Deneham was the younger son of a baron and before he married was admired greatly for his good looks and charm. Debutantes smiled and fluttered their eyelashes to get his attention, hoping he would ask them to dance at the balls. They saved spaces on their dance cards for him and cried of a broken heart when their parents refused his request to pay his addresses to them. Until Sir Marcus met Lady Alexandra Hurst, he thought he was going to have to find employment to earn his living, since without a title or fortune to recommend him, he was unlikely to contract a *marriage of convenience*.

Lady Alexandra was the Earl of Halifax's only child and entered her first Season of balls and fetes with exuberance. She owned a large enough dowry that her common face and figure were initially overlooked by the noblemen flocking to make her acquaintance, until they learned she spoke with a loud and resonating voice. She tried not to cry when they quickly took their leave of her to make their way to another debutante who, unlike herself, was the epitome of demure. One evening, alone, without friend or suitor to distract her, she blushed from embarrassment upon hearing the unkind words being said about her manner. Hoping her absence would desist their assault on her person, she skirted the dance floor to make her way to the card room where she hoped to find her father. Her hostess intercepted her before she could escape the ballroom and informed her the handsome man at her side wished to be introduced to her. Marcus Deneham grinned at her surprised look and greeted her with alacrity. Lady Alexandra was so captivated by the man's good looks and friendly nature, that she did not even notice when their hostess left them. Marcus's engaging manner quickly pulled her out of her doldrums and into high spirits. She was thoroughly enjoying herself, listening to him recollect the last time he attended the opera, while she recalled her own visit. Before she knew it, her voice rose in excitement. When she saw Mr. Deneham was ready to erupt in laugher, she balked and covered her hand over her mouth in mortification. She expected him, like the other gentlemen, to abandon her. Instead, he told her not to stop for he wanted to hear the rest of her tale. In that moment she felt Cupid's arrow.

Meg knew, regardless of the gossip, her parents held a deep affection for one another. Over the years, she had never seen anything but adoration between them. She knew marriages were contracted for mutual benefit and while no one doubted her mother's dowry had been enticing, she did not believe that was the only reason her father had married her mother. He was no charlatan. Even though he had led an indulgent life, he was far from indolent. He was smart, making investments, that over time tripled her mother's fortune. His success and innate shrewdness drew others to him for business advice. Even the Prince Regent sought his counsel and knighted him for his invaluable service to the crown. Generous to a fault, Meg could never remember a time when her father did not grant her every wish, nor could she remember him ever uttering a harsh word to her or her mother. Even when others looked disapprovingly at his wife's boisterous manner, she never once saw her father chastise her mother for it. In fact, on more than one occasion, Meg saw her father rally to her mother's defense with a charm that managed to appease everyone's ego. There was no doubt in Meg's mind Sir Marcus loved his wife.

As the Denehams entered the parlour, Meg noted they were the first to arrive. She blushed when she saw Lord Atwood frown upon seeing her. She regretted she had ever teased him and was even sorrier her repartee had destroyed any chance of him admiring her. She could not deny she liked him. He was a handsome man having lost his boyish countenance from when they first met two years ago. He looked strong and fit. She guessed he had joined the Corinthian set of gentlemen who engaged in pugilism and other sporting pursuits. He had a square jawline, discerning eyes, and a confident stance. She found him thoroughly beguiling with his light-brown hair and whiskey-brown eyes. As she took in his elegant attire her anger volleyed between being mad at herself for initially teasing him and at him for holding onto a grudge. *"For heaven's sake,"* she thought. *"It has been two years. Will he never forgive nor forget?"*

Meg followed her parents to make her greeting. When she faced Lord Atwood, she feared he would give her the *cut direct* and intentionally ignore her, so to ameliorate him, she offered up her friendliest smile. However, her cheerful effort only seemed to deepen the scowl that originated when he first saw her enter the room.

She was further discommoded when her parents drew Lord and Lady Felton away in conversation and she was left to engage the scowling viscount into the niceties of parlour speech. She girded herself against the man who seemed to dislike her with a passion. Pulling from her reservoir of innocuous questions she used for parlour banter, she asked, "Are you enjoying the Season, my lord?"

"Yes."

Lawrence hated hearing the sharp tone of his reply. It was so out of character for him to be abrupt, but he found he was always on guard when he was in Meg's company, waiting for her to make him the jest of her joke. Every time the corners of her mouth turned up in a smile, he remembered his embarrassment and his temper rose. He wished he could simply ignore her, but it was difficult when the lady was pretty and always in happy spirits. She was wearing a flattering high-waist rose silk dress with puffy sleeves that accentuated her slender yet abundant womanly features. Her rich dark hair was styled in a becoming coif with curls framing her bright-eyed face. Her brown eyes sparkled with laughter. Whether he was the center of her amusement or not, Lawrence found himself totally captivated by her.

Meg watched Lord Atwood blatantly examine her person and she started to blush at his intense stare. She breathed in a cleansing breath to regain her wits and then hoped to halt his inspection of her by distracting him with her chatter. She recalled her shopping on Bond Street, her repast at Fortnum and Mason, and finally her visit to Hatchard's, where she explained with the sudden wave of her arm, the store's multitude of books. To her mortification, her arm clipped, not too softly, his nose.

She screamed when he stepped back from her assault to cover his injured face with his hands. Her outcry drew everyone's attention, including Lord Felton's newly arrived company: the Earl and Countess of Westfield and Mr. Kevin Donahue. Embarrassed at being made a spectacle, Lawrence quickly removed a piece of linen from the inside of his coat pocket and applied it to his bleeding nose. He nodded to the newly arrived guests, mumbling, "Excuse me," while he hastily made his exit.

Lady Felton exclaimed, "Oh, dear!" While Lady Deneham asked her daughter, "Meg, Did you injure Lord Atwood?"

Meg crimsoned at having to acknowledge her humiliation, "Only by accident, Mama."

"If it was anything else, I am sure you had your reasons."

Kevin Donahue could not refrain from grinning. He made his way to Meg and to the horror of her parents introduced himself to her. Unsure how to respond under her parents' watchful eyes, Meg was thankful when the Earl of Felton came to her aid.

"Allow me to properly present our guest, Miss Deneham. He hails from America and I fear he is unaware it is ill-mannered of him to make his own introduction."

Edward continued, "Miss Deneham, it is my honor to introduce Mr. Kevin Donahue to you, recently arrived from America. Mr. Donahue, please meet Miss Margaret Deneham, daughter of Sir Marcus and Lady Deneham, who are also anxious to make your acquaintance."

"It is a pleasure to meet you, Miss Deneham," he greeted. "I do beg your forgiveness. His lordship is correct in that I am unaware of the rules of English Society. Where I am from, it is considered unneighborly not to introduce oneself."

"Ah!" gasped Meg, who was mesmerized by the robust blond-haired, blue-eyed man. She had never met an American and was ready to ask him about his home when Lawrence returned.

"Lord Atwood," hailed Kevin with enthusiasm. "I see you are unscathed. I commend your fortitude." He proffered his hand and when Lawrence grabbed hold of it, Kevin slapped him on the back with his other hand and let out the laugh he had stifled earlier. Lawrence could not refrain from joining him.

Edward chided, "Let us not forget decorum, Mr. Donahue. I insist we finish our introductions."

Kevin released another chuckle, "I am deservingly chastised, my lord. I hope my new friends will continue to guide me as I enter your convoluted society."

No sooner were the introductions properly made than Simmons announced dinner was served. Their host, the Earl of Felton, led the way into the dining parlour with Lady Westfield on his arm, while Lord Westfield followed them, escorting the earl's wife, Lady Felton. Viscount Atwood allowed the inferior ranking Sir Marcus Deneham and his wife to precede him and escorted along with Mr. Kevin Donahue, Miss Margaret Deneham.

Lawrence looked forward to sitting next to Kevin to learn about the man's travels and homeland. Kevin would sit to the right of Lord Felton as guest of honor and Lawrence planned to take the seat on his other side, so he was not pleased when Meg took the covetous spot which forced him to sit next to her. He felt a pang of envy when Kevin and Meg fell into a light and cheerful conversation. He did not particularly like the ease that existed between them. He could not understand why, aside from himself, everyone got along quite nicely with the young lady. He counseled himself to check his temper, so as not to draw unwanted attention to himself.

Jonathan was the first to prod Mr. Donahue on his family connections, "How long has your family lived in America?"

"My mother's family came over with a land grant in the 1670's, so they predate the revolution. My grandfather, Sean Donahue, was pressed into serving his majesty's army in 1773. He was five and ten years old when he was forced onto one of his majesty's ships headed for America."

"Oh!" gasped Meg. "His family must have been fraught with worry wondering what happened to him."

"I believe they had all passed at the time. My grandfather left Ireland after the black disease hit his village. He only survived because he was away on a hunting trip when his family fell ill. When he returned, his mother would not let him enter the family hut. His last memory of home was his mother tossing him what little coin she had from the doorway. With no place to go, he boarded one of the skiffs making its way to England."

"Do you mean to say he left for England with no one to help him once he arrived?" asked Anne.

"Indeed, I believe his mother told him to get as far away as possible. He was seeking work down by the London docks when he was swooped up in a raid and pressed into military service."

"Do they still use press-gangs, Marcus?" inquired his wife.

"It is not unheard for the navy to recruit by force, Alexandra, when they are short on manpower."

Appalled, Meg ranted, "But he was only five and ten years old!"

"Most midshipmen begin their training at three and ten years, Miss Deneham," remarked Jonathan. "Besides, what has age to do with anything. Our textile factories are filled with children doing a man's job. I expect he looked strong enough to serve and so was recruited."

"I thought Mr. Donahue said he was forced," questioned Alexandra.

"He was," explained Kevin, "but once captured, he preferred to take the king's coin and be paid for his service, than serve without pay. That is the only difference between being recruited and pressed into service."

Meg wanted to inquire more about the children working in the factories, but kept her questions to herself when the earl asked Mr. Donahue another question. She did not wish to detour the conversation into a subject that seemed to upset Lord Westfield, so she remained silent.

Jonathan asked, "How did your grandfather remain in America, Mr. Donahue?"

"He followed the drum for two years before falling sick with a camp fever. He was unable to keep up, so he was left behind at the farm where his troop billeted for the night. The farmer's daughter nursed him and over time, they fell in love. Needless to say, Sean Donahue married her and never returned to his troop or England."

Meg's eyes sparkled, "I am sorry for your grandfather's loss and hardship, but to know he prevailed makes for a happy tale."

"He often said Providence steered his course."

"I believe you mentioned, Mr. Donahue," queried Jonathan, "that your family business is in tobacco. I was wondering whether you utilized the use of slaves in harvesting your crop?"

Kevin's cheery disposition altered immediately. He responded sternly, "No, my lord. We do not own slaves. My grandfather, pressed into service, was set against any philosophy that takes a man's will away from him. My father is of the same belief."

The earl smiled, "I must confess I am glad to hear it and will admit we are of the same mind."

Elinor, in an effort to lighten the heavy mood, asked, "You mentioned a sister to my husband, Mr. Donahue. Do you have any other siblings?"

"I have a younger brother, Ryan, Dr. Donahue to be precise. He works at the General Hospital in Boston."

"And your sister?" asked Anne. "I understand from my husband she is to be married."

"Indeed, I am tasked to purchase her bridal cloth." Kevin turned to ask Meg, "Perhaps you could assist me, Miss Deneham. I am sure you know the best drapers and I have no doubt you have impeccable taste."

Meg's eyes widened with glee, "I would be delighted to help you, Mr. Donahue. I know just where to take you. When would you like to go?"

Meg reminded Kevin of his sister Katie. She had no pretensions about herself and was full of energy. He liked how she made no effort to flirt with him or to get him to attend to her through the use of schemes. She did not seek flattery or the center of attention, even though her beauty and manner worked against her wishes. Kevin thought they would get along well.

"Would tomorrow be too soon?"

Meg turned to look at her mother for permission and was pleased to see her give it with a slight nod. She turned back to Kevin and gave her answer, "Not at all, Mr. Donahue, I will be ready. Shall we say one o'clock?"

Kevin had hoped for an earlier start, but then he remembered the aristocracy rarely rose before noon. He agreed to the time and then asked Lawrence, "Perhaps, my lord, you could direct me to a good livery, so I can rent the use of a carriage for the day."

"Nonsense, my day is free. Allow me to accompany you both. I have my own carriage in Town and would be happy to be of service to you."

Lawrence saw Meg's eyes widen in surprise and wondered if he expressed the same astonishment in his own features. He could not believe he just offered to spend the day with her, especially when her manner almost always provoked him, but somehow the idea of Mr. Donahue and Miss Deneham engaged in an afternoon together without benefit of a proper chaperone perturbed him more than her manner. He knew Lady Deneham, as propriety dictated, would have Meg's maid accompany her. However, Lawrence was experienced enough to know a maid, a subservient, offered little deterrence to a gentleman determined to take liberties with a young lady, especially if that young lady was willing. Hadn't he snatched a kiss or two under such chaperonage? The question provoking him was whether Meg was willing?

Lawrence's nagging curiosity compelled him to lean forward on the dining table and scrutinize the engaging couple. He focused wholeheartedly on them to discover their intentions. He examined them to see if they were actively flirting with one another or simply enjoying each other's company. He must have looked fretful because when Meg turned to face him, she exclaimed, "My lord, is something wrong? You look quite put out!"

Her boisterous comment drew everyone's notice to him and he had to hold his tongue and not give Miss Deneham the verbal lashing she deserved for once again bringing undue attention to him. He felt ridiculous having everyone gawk at him, but he was no longer the inexperienced boy for whom Meg could chase away with her teasing. He gained enough life experience traveling abroad to turn the table on anyone trying to discommode him. He took a calming breath, before replying, "Not at all, Miss Deneham. If I seemed alarmed, it was only for the safety of Mr. Donahue. Your hands seem to take on a life of their own when you speak and I was sure Mr. Donahue was about to be assaulted."

"You are too magnanimous, my lord," feigned Meg. "But I am sure Mr. Donahue can take care of himself."

Kevin laughed, "I don't know Miss Deneham. I have seen you draw blood. I would be grateful to his lordship for any protection he might grant me."

Meg dropped her jaw in mortification, feeling the warmth of a blush rise up her neck. She saw Lawrence's tight lips widen into a grin and before indignation could set in, laughter abounded around the table sparking her own giggles to escape her mouth.

Chapter Four

Atwood's elegant carriage halted in front of the venerable George Inn and before Lawrence could command his footman with his wishes, Kevin Donahue opened the carriage door, jumped inside and took a seat opposite him. Lawrence's surprise at having the American jump into his coach turned to amusement when he saw how much Mr. Donahue admired his luxurious coach.

"This is quite an ostentatious ride, Atwood. I have not seen anything like it before."

"Until two years ago, neither had I."

The comment peaked Kevin's interest and he queried his lordship by raising an eyebrow.

Lawrence laughed, "It is true. I only became aware of my aristocratic lineage upon the death of my mother. I learned I was the only surviving male in the Atwood family line to inherit. My grandmother in her youth married a military man her family disapproved. Her father wanted her to marry a titled man of wealth. He was so angry with her that when she eloped he cut her out of the family. However, when he learned her husband died in action, he asked her to return home, thinking he could finally contract a marriage from which he could profit. My grandmother had just given birth to my mother and she feared her father would think her child made her less desirable. She knew her father had no scruples and out of fear for my mother's safety, my grandmother went into hiding. She relocated and changed her name, so her father could not find her. The sad part of the story is her husband did not die in action and when he came to look for her, my great-grandfather, told him she died in childbirth. I later learned, unknown to them, they both lived their lives in seaside towns within twenty miles of each other."

"That is a heartwrenching story, my lord, and I am sorry for your loss. Tell me, how did you become aware of your inheritance upon your mother's death?"

"My grandmother and mother raised me to be a proper gentleman and had me tutored as one. Looking back, I should have questioned their motive, for while I received an education equal to any child of the realm, I owned no skill to make my way in the world. Upon my mother's death, I found myself penniless and alone. I owe Beaumont and Felton for all my good fortune, for even before my identity was learned, they embraced me kindly, a stranger who appeared on their doorstep with nothing to recommend him but his grandmother's name."

"You were a stranger to Beaumont?"

"Yes, but my grandmother always mentioned him with affection. She told me if I ever needed help, I could seek him out and so I did."

"A true rags to riches story. Do you like being titled and living among the aristocracy?" Before Lawrence could answer, Kevin added, "You must forgive me, but I have found most of them more haughty than not."

"Indeed, but once you break into our sphere, you will find there are many great and honorable families you cannot but approve. Lords Beaumont, Felton, Westfield, Ingall, Hartford have been great supporters and friends of mine. You have met some of them." Remembering his duty, he exclaimed, "Ah! I almost forgot. I am charged to deliver a missive to you."

Lawrence opened his greatcoat and removed the letter from his inner pocket. He handed it to Kevin who looked at the sealed note with caution, as if fearful to open it, "Do you know what is inside?"

Mr. Donahue's concern made Lawrence chuckle, "Nothing devious, I assure you."

Kevin broke the wax seal that had the imprint of Felton's signet ring and read:

Dear Mr. Donahue,

I am most interested in discussing a business venture with you and since I am doubly interested in furthering our acquaintance, I would find it most agreeable if you would quit the George Inn and finish your stay in London as my guest. I expect nothing less than your agreement and so have taken the liberty to alert Lady Montague you will be accompanying us to her ball this evening. I look forward to seeing you then.

Felton

"He will not take no for an answer?"

"Indeed not."

They fell into easy banter, sharing interests and making plans to indulge in some of London's entertainments when to their surprise the carriage stopped.

"It appears, Mr. Donahue, we are here."

"Then, I suggest, my lord, we not keep the redoubtable Miss Deneham waiting."

They quickly debarked from the carriage, feeling in good humor with one another, and walked up the steps to the Deneham town home. Lawrence removed a calling card from his silver case and had it ready to proffer to the Deneham butler. He was not surprised to gain entry and be bid welcome as the Denehams were not sticklers to Society's rules of conduct. Normally, Lawrence would wait for the butler to inquire whether their master was *at home* to receive him. It was the way of the *ton* to filter their visitors, refusing entry to those they deemed unworthy by simply having their butler say they were not *at home*. The Denehams did not adhere to the protocol. Everyone knew if their butler said the Denehams were not at home, then they were indeed not at home.

Lawrence liked the Deneham's affable nature, but he knew the *bon ton* did not, often chiding them for their lax standards. He knew Lady Deneham's wealth and connections kept her family from being shunned by polite society. Her clout gave her family a pass for their uncommon manner and more times than not, they were simply marked *Original.*

Viscount Atwood and Mr. Donahue followed the butler into the foyer and were surprised to hear Meg's voice. They both turned in time to see her walking down the stairs with her abigail following behind her. She looked quite fetching in her azure *Gros de Naples* pelisse and bonnet. A blue satin ribbon tied loosely under her neck framed her jovial face. She remarked cheerfully, "I see I was correct. I knew you would arrive punctually, neither two minutes early, nor two minutes late."

At that moment, the long case clock gracing the wall nearby chimed once. While Kevin laughed at her remark, Lawrence frowned. He was sure Meg was making fun of him, "You give us too much credit, Miss Deneham."

Mr. Donahue's resounding chuckles overrode the sting of Lord Atwood's words and Meg smiled. She was encouraged by the American's obvious approval and suggested to them, "Since we are on a very personal expedition, shopping for betrothal linen for Mr. Donahue's sister, do you not think it would be more conducive for us to use our Christian names and you could call me Meg."

"It would be my pleasure, Meg, as long as you call me Kevin."

Meg noticed Lord Atwood's scowl, but decided to press on anyway, "And will you follow suit, my lord?"

Kevin turned to look at Lawrence who did not reply readily. He gave him an elbow to the ribs which evoked the viscount to respond. Lawrence shrugged off his disgruntlement, "Very well, Meg. Shall we go?"

Lawrence and Kevin allowed Meg to precede them when the Deneham butler opened the door. Kevin was about to let her abigail pass as well, but the woman kept her distance with her eyes cast down. Lawrence noticed the American's chagrin, "She is her maid, Donahue. She is expected to be invisible unless needed. Do not extend the same courtesies to her as you would a lady of quality. You will only cause her embarrassment and make her afraid of being reprimanded. You see, a maid who draws a gentleman's attention could be severely punished or released without a reference."

"You are not serious."

"Indeed, I am. Our social class system is distinct. Even the serving class has its own levels of rank to be respected."

With that said, Kevin and Lawrence exited the Deneham town home with Meg's abigail trailing in their wake. As the footman opened the carriage door for Lord Atwood's party, Lawrence gave his coachman their direction.

Before entering the carriage, Meg interrupted, "My lord, not Bond Street. We are off to Cheapside."

The coachman, upon hearing Miss Deneham's direction, looked to his master for his orders. Lawrence nodded his approval and then followed his guests into the carriage. He noticed Mr. Donahue was courteous to take the seat with his back to the horses which would allow Meg's maid, when she entered, to sit next to her mistress and face forward. He took the seat next to him and saw Meg smile at his own consideration for her maid's comfort. He felt ridiculously embarrassed by her notice.

No sooner had the door slammed shut when they felt the coach jerk forward. They traveled in comfort seated on plush velveteen squabs and felt nothing more than a gentle sway from the well-sprung carriage while they made their way down Oxford Street. Once they left the fashionable district of London, Lawrence pulled down his window shade and then leaned over to pull down the shade to cover the window where Kevin was taking in the sights. Lawrence's action surprised the American and before Kevin could ask him what he was about by shutting out his view, Meg explained, "Lord Atwood is being gallant, Mr. Donahue. He is shielding my innocent eyes from the disturbing sight of Newgate Prison and the unsavory residents who walk these streets. While you will find Cheapside packed with members of our elevated society, you will not find them loitering on this thoroughfare. Did you know Cheapside has been a hub for shopping since medieval times. The name itself is an old name for barter."

"I did not know that and I thought you were going to call me Kevin."

"How silly of me to forget, especially since it was my idea." Meg looked at Lawrence with her bright brown eyes, "Do not think I do not appreciate your consideration, Lawrence. It was most thoughtful of you to shield my sensibilities."

Much to Lawrence's chagrin, he smiled at her acknowledgement. When the horses started to slow their pace, he raised the carriage blind to see if they had arrived at their destination. He could see Cheapside, home to two and three story merchant warehouses, had already drawn a flurry of activity. The sidewalks were crushed with pedestrians, from all walks of life meandering the street, looking through storefront windows for the latest bonnet, crockery, or snuff box.

Lawrence grimaced looking at the congested thoroughfare, "We are here and as usual it is a crush. I suggest we debark and let my man find a place to park my carriage until we are ready to leave. Do you think an hour will suffice?"

Meg inquired of Mr. Donahue, "Are we only purchasing linen today or is there more on your list?"

Kevin chuckled, "I was only charged with the purchase of linen, Meg. Has my mother been remiss in not asking for more?"

"No, of course not. I just was not sure if you wanted matching slippers and gloves or perhaps a bonnet or two."

"I assure you, Meg, my sister would be forever in your debt, if you would purchase whatever you deem necessary."

Meg joyfully clasped her hands, "How fun! We will start with the drapers. Please have your coachman halt, my lord. We have arrived at my favorite merchant."

Lawrence pounded the roof to alert his coachman he wished to stop. He then asked again, "Will an hour suffice, Meg?"

She laughed, "No, my lord. I suggest your man return in two hours. If we finish early, we can enjoy a small repast."

Meg enthusiastically made her way from one shop to another. She was very excited to be of service to Mr. Donahue and while Kevin found her lively behavior amusing, Lawrence found it worrisome at best. Even though Meg moved with grace, he knew those hands of hers could be lethal. He feared she was destined for a catastrophe.

The time passed quickly visiting one warehouse after another. Lawrence was amazed Meg's energy did not diminish as the hour came and passed. He watched her enter another store. This time to his pleasure he was allowed to wait outside, while she selected those unmentionables women found so dear. Kevin's eye caught the sign of a tobacco shop across the street and suggested they investigate it while Meg made her purchases. Lawrence declined, feeling honor-bound to wait for Meg where he said he would be. Kevin crossed the street to browse, promising to return soon.

Lawrence shook his head from side to side. He never would have thought to find himself waiting outside a lingerie shop for a woman who constantly managed to discomfit him. Meg had him vigilant from the moment they debarked his coach. They had entered her favorite merchant's shop, renowned for its large selection of cloth and superior service. Rows of divided shelves, forming boxes, covered both sides of the walls. From each cubby hole, hung a colorful swath of material. Bright yellows, greens, blues, reds, and brilliant whites in all manner of material draped the wall like a parade of flags. Behind the counters were several young male clerks attending customers, showing them sample books of linen and colored fashion plates. In the center of the room were a number of large tables where a clerk worked at one table to cut a swath of material for a customer. Lawrence was pleased to see the store was thin on patrons and he hoped Meg could make her purchases with haste. The idea of a speedy conclusion banished quickly when Meg called a clerk by name. *"Clearly"*, he thought, *"she spends a great deal of time here if she knows the clerks by name."* He had to stifle a chuckle when he saw how quickly the clerk's cheerful manner subdued when he saw it was Miss Deneham beckoning him.

Before long, the young tradesman was scurrying up and down the ladders resting against the wooden shelves like a shipboard mouse. Up and down, the young man went, retrieving various bolts of cloth. Lawrence was getting tired just watching him. The clerk's pristine demeanor began to wane as beads of sweat collected at his hairline and slowly gravitated down the side of his face to find a resting place inside his cravat. He looked withered and in need of a respite. As the man placed another bolt of sprigged muslin on the table, Lawrence asked Meg, "Why do you not simply make your selection from the sample book like the other patrons?"

Meg's eyes widened, "My lord, the samples are too small and it is difficult to know if they are indeed flattering. I need to drape them and overlay the muslins and the sarsnets to see what works best. I would be remiss if I did not put the same attention in making selections for Miss Donahue as I would for myself."

Impressed by her sincerity, he apologized, "I stand corrected, Meg. Forgive my intrusion."

He continued to watch in amazement while Meg directed the clerk to retrieve bolts of cloth. He worried over her tendency to hover at the foot of the ladder where the man climbed and feared for her safety each time the worker pulled on the rolled cloth above her head. When he saw Meg try to step up the ladder, he swiftly grasped her waist and brusquely pulled her back into his body. She hit his chest and gasped at his roughness. Lawrence scolded, "Stop, Meg. You will refrain from collecting the linen yourself."

Incensed at being manhandled and unduly reprimanded, Meg turned and was ready to release a scathing put down, until she saw the fear in Lawrence's eyes. His concern for her safety took her breath away and instead of a cutting remark, she whispered, "Thank you, my lord. I fear I was not thinking."

Surprised by her candor, Lawrence beamed with gladness and acknowledged her appreciation, "You are most welcome, Meg."

Meg noticed Lord Atwood was even more attractive when he smiled. She took in his rich brown eyes, his straight nose, and his provocative mouth. She grinned back at him and saw him immediately flatten his lips, step back from her and inspect their surroundings. Her high spirits returned when she realized he was not angry with her, but with himself for putting her character into question with his closeness. She wanted to hug him for being protective and sweet. Luckily, before she made a fool of herself, the clerk shouted, "Is this the correct sarsnet, Miss Deneham?"

Lawrence came out of his reflection when he heard Meg's laughter. He immediately became concerned when he saw she was not watching where she was going. Her attention was on her abigail who was struggling with the multiple packages she carried. He heard Meg giggle trying to grab one of the slipping parcels from the maid's stack. She was so preoccupied with her task she failed to be chary exiting the shop. The sidewalk was crushed with pedestrians. Meg no sooner stepped outside than a passing gentleman ran into her shoulder, causing her to stumble backwards. The offender walked on his way without an apology or thought to Meg, cursing her beneath his breath.

Lawrence stepped in front of the boorish man, "I believe you owe the lady an apology for your inconsideration."

The man balked and retorted, "It was not I who caused the collision. The lady, if she is one, was not watching where she was going."

Lawrence instinctively reacted to the man's insult, drew back his fist and struck him in the face.

"Bloody hell," the man cried, bringing his hands up to cover his bleeding face, "I think you have broken my nose."

"It seems you failed to watch where you were going and walked right into my fist."

Without another thought to the man's distress, Lawrence went to collect Meg who was watching with a gaping mouth in astonishment. He brought his hands to cup her face which reminded her to close her mouth. Looking into her widened eyes, he asked, "Are you hurt?"

"Not at all," and then she watched while her gallant straightened her bonnet and threaded her hand through his arm. Ignoring the crowd, who had assembled to gawk at the man with the bloody nose, they proceeded down the street towards a hawker selling meat pies. Smiling, Lawrence asked, "Are you hungry?"

"Yes," she replied wearing an unfashionably large smile.

Chapter Five

Meg stared into her mirror while her abigail completed the finishing touches on her coiffure. She half listened to her maid's remarks because her own thoughts distracted her.

"That *facer* he delivered was something wasn't it, miss? I mean who would have thought?"

Meg smiled at her maid's reflection, "Yes, Mary. He was quite chivalrous. I cannot recall having anyone fight for me before. Usually my gentlemen friends are chiding me for not being aware of my surroundings."

"Well, you do tend to get excited, but that is neither here nor there. That nasty man ran into you without one word of regret. I think it mighty honorable of his lordship to settle it the way he did. I hope the bloody man's nose heals crooked. Would serve him right!"

Meg laughed, rising, she looked at her maid and agreeably replied, "Indeed."

Mary grinned back at her mistress, proud they were of the same mind in the matter of Lord Atwood. She stepped back to better view her handiwork and was quite happy with her results. She complimented her mistress's beauty and then asked her which wrap she preferred to wear, the Belgian lace or the Indian silk.

Lawrence rode in his own carriage with Kevin, while the Earl and Countess of Felton preceded them in their own distinguished chaise. Lawrence was glad he suggested taking two carriages to the Montague Ball in the event the *enceinte* Lady Felton wished to leave the festivities early. He was even happier his friends bore no witness to Kevin's continued remarks on his earlier folly in Cheapside.

"I wish I had seen it. I was told you had him with one bloody punch."

"Enough!" scolded Lawrence. "You have enjoyed sufficient entertainment at my expense. You know very well I was obligated to intervene. After all, Miss Deneham, was under my protection."

Lawrence's outburst amused Kevin. Grinning, he placated, "Of course, my lord, you acted superbly and I am sure Miss Deneham is all gratitude."

"You are a scoundrel, Donahue, I expect, as a man of honor, you will ensure Miss Deneham is not made the jest of anyone's jokes this evening because of my rash behavior."

"You need not fear for Miss Deneham, However, I expect your name to be bantered about this evening, O Gallant One."

And so it was. No sooner did Lawrence enter the ballroom did he hear the titters of *gossipmongers*. He found himself being congratulated by the young bucks and flattered by the newly presented debutantes. He was accosted with slaps to his back and a flutter of fans covering the grins of admiring ladies. More than one lady's flagrant stare and nod of appreciation caught his attention. The crush and display being made on his behalf became intolerable. He barely heard Kevin say, "I will see you later. I am off to the card room," before the man left.

He accepted a few more accolades before escaping himself. He found a secluded spot behind an Ionic pillar and potted fern from where he could quietly observe the ballroom without being accosted. The leafy plant shielded him from onlookers, as well as, the gentlemen who stood on the other side of the column. It seemed their eyes were also on the dance floor.

"Who are you seeking, Spencer?"

"A fortune."

"Seriously, Spencer. I heard you were paying court to Lady Barrett. Is that not going well?"

"Too slow for my taste, Grantham. I need to fill my coffers now, not in six months. I don't suppose you have any suggestions?"

At that moment, the set ended and the dancers dispersed. Lawrence saw Meg being escorted back to her mother's side by a respectable looking gentleman and he realized he had not just been watching the dancing, but had been searching for her. He felt his gut tighten when the man brushed his lips over Meg's hand in farewell. He was halfway across the empty dance floor before he became aware he was making his way to Meg. His determined stride was remarked upon and by the time he reached her, the ballroom was filled with resounding chatter. He saw Meg blush when he came to a stop in front of her and he heard his name echo with the words "lovesick" and "fool."

He crimsoned in embarrassment understanding the speculation he just initiated by almost acknowledging Meg before her mother. Since he had no wish for his name to be bantered about in tomorrow's parlours, he immediately turned his attention to Meg's mother, "Good evening, Lady Deneham."

Alexandra grinned at the discomfited viscount and returned her own salutation along with her thanks, "Good evening, my lord. I understand I owe you a debt of gratitude in coming to my daughter's aid. You will come to dinner tomorrow, so my husband and I may bestow our appreciation properly."

Lawrence knew better than to argue. A dinner invitation was a common courtesy and to refuse it would be considered gauche, so he accepted the request.

"You may bring your American friend."

"Thank you, Lady Deneham. I am sure Mr. Donahue will be delighted to come."

Lawrence finally turned to look at Meg and saw her face brighten immediately at his attention. He boyishly grinned in return until he heard the burgeoning chatter, reminding him he was on display. His cheerful disposition turned fretful and he realized when Meg's beaming smile flattened in distress that she was as poor as himself in hiding her feelings. He attempted to make amends for his peaked temper by requesting to dance the next set with her and his mood improved when she agreed. He bowed and took his leave until he could claim his dance, disappointing the spectators who watched the young couple for amusement.

He crossed the ballroom and made his way to the card room feeling his embarrassment spike again when he saw all the smirks and grins thrown his way. He hated being fodder for the *gossipmongers*, but could blame no one but himself for the unwanted attention. It was unlike him to act impulsively and yet within one day, he broke the nose of a lout and mooned over a debutante. He wished he owned a monocle, so like many of the noblemen, he could use it to stare down his nose at those peers who dared to banter his name about. The Marquis of Beaumont taught him to never let anyone know when he was upset. Indifference, he said, was the greatest weapon against those who wished to best him with words. He realized it would be impossible to feel indifferent when he was around Meg.

Lawrence was so deep in his thoughts he did not see Edward approach him until his lordship patted him on the shoulder to gain his attention. He whispered, "You must not let them see that they can affect you. They are looking for amusement and your obvious vexation with them is satisfying them well."

"It seems I have yet to completely master that uncaring manner that seems to be bred into you aristocrats."

"Trust me, it is a learned trait and one that will serve you well."

"Do you always remain unaffected?"

"To be honest, no, but I have no desire to give anyone power over me. I am too selfish and spiteful a man to give anyone so great a gift."

Lawrence laughed, "You are one of the kindest and generous of men I know, Felton, but I heed your warning. I shall check my emotions and try to keep from making a spectacle of myself with Miss Deneham."

"It is smart not to let others read you like a book, nor let others manipulate your actions. Your feelings for Miss Deneham are yours alone to do with as you please. If you allow society to influence your behavior, then you have no one to blame but yourself for the consequences. I would never be happily married, if I had allowed the *ton* to dictate my choice of wife."

"Wife!" choked Lawrence. "For heaven's sake, Felton. I have offered a dance for the lady, nothing more, and in that I am beginning to regret."

"That is a shame, Atwood. Miss Deneham is an undiscovered treasure. I know her exuberant manner has kept many from offering for her, but eventually someone coveting her large dowry will court her to gain it." Edward saw his wife without company and excused himself to go to her.

Lawrence reflected on his lordship's words while he went to find Mr. Donahue in the card room. He was happy to see the American owned a pile of coins and was engaging in an amiable discussion.

"Atwood!" exclaimed Kevin. "Your timing is fortuitous. What do you say we extend our apologies to our hosts and make our way to the clubs. The luck is with me tonight and I am looking for higher stakes."

Lawrence knew he should have refused, but he saw a means of escape and leaped at the chance. He did not know how he felt towards Meg and he did not want his behavior misconstrued. While he felt bad to renege on their dance, he felt justified he was doing the right thing. He had no desire for her to think of him as a suitor, so he flagged a footman for pen and paper to write a note of regrets, explaining to her he was unable to claim his dance. He promised in his note to call on her the next day. Before taking his leave with Mr. Donahue, he commanded a servant to deliver his note.

Meg had just declined Lord Spencer's invitation to dance when a footman delivered Lord Atwood's letter. She unfolded the unsealed message and as she read his news, her smile faltered. Lord Spencer noted her sadness, "I hope it is not ill news, Miss Deneham. Is there anything I can do?"

"It seems, my lord, I am available to dance after all, if that is still your pleasure."

"It is indeed." He offered Meg his arm and smugly escorted her onto the dance floor.

Meg was sorely disappointed Lawrence was called away, having wished to become better acquainted with him. They spent what she thought was a lovely afternoon in Cheapside sharing a camaraderie over the day's events. She knew she liked to be in his company and after their excursion had hoped he felt the same way.

But of course, that was before the *gossipmongers* spread the story of his gallantry. She remembered how uncomfortable he was at being speculated about and she feared he would abandon furthering any acquaintance with her.

She could not help but compare Lord Spencer with Lord Atwood as they took their positions on the dance floor. Spencer was older than Lawrence, at least ten years his senior, and like Lawrence, he was a handsome and well-figured man, though he owned a crop of blond hair and blue eyes to Lawrence's brown hair and brown eyes. Meg knew Spencer was popular with many women who blatantly vied for his favor. He was a renowned charmer and owned eyes that always seemed to gleam in amusement. Those eyes usually broke through a lady's reserve, but Meg thought he looked like someone with mischief on his mind. His practiced air was very unlike Lawrence who lacked any form of pretense.

Comparisons aside, Meg knew she did not like Spencer's posturing and his proprietary manner, acting as though he had authority over her. His flagrant attention unnerved her and made her wonder why he was pressing his advances upon her, since he had never shown an interest in her before. While she knew she should feel flattered, her instincts were screaming for her to be wary. She wished Lawrence was her partner instead of the imposing Lord Spencer. The viscount's absence plagued her and she began to worry if Lawrence was truly called away or if his note was a ruse to escape her company.

It did not take long for Spencer to realize Meg was not paying an iota of attention to him. In fact, her far-off stare suggested she did not even see him. Usually, he found it easy to seduce a young debutante into believing she was in love with him. He only had to offer soft words and smiles, but Meg's eyes were dull and disengaged from his company and after his third unsuccessful attempt at flirtation his temper began to rise. He wanted to slap her as one might shock a hysterical person back to their senses, but he feared she would not react as he wished. No doubt, the lady would scream and accuse him of assault. Her father would come to her aid and forbid him from her company. The last thing he needed was to be seen as a villain. On the contrary, he needed Miss Deneham's good opinion for them to marry.

Chapter Six

Lawrence used his silver-tipped walking stick to tap on the Deneham's door. The Malacca cane was a recent purchase and he felt proud as a peacock to own the exotic piece of wood. The walking stick was crafted specifically for him out of cane wood imported from the strait of Malacca in Malaysia. The imported wood, harvested from the stem of a rattan palm, owned a smooth and glossy brown finish. Lawrence had his cane topped off with a silver knob engraved with his family's crest. He thought his walking stick rather conservative to others crafted to represent animal heads or automatons where the head moved upon the touch of a button. He could have chosen gold, ivory, or even bejeweled his knob, but found the style too gaudy and pretentious for himself.

He ran his thumb over the silver knob while he waited for his tattoo on the door to be answered by a servant and recalled the sword sheathed within the cane's hollow wood. He felt the little button where if pressed released a sword he could use to protect himself should he be accosted. The lethal swordstick was the weapon of choice for the noble to carry for it did not encumber the gentleman or distract from his attire.

He had spent the last two years honing his defensive skills. He was not a master but capable enough. His workouts with both Lords Felton and Westfield had wielded his slender frame into a sinewy body. When provoked, he could be an intimidating opponent.

He tugged on his embroidered waistcoat while he waited for the Deneham butler to open the door. He hoped his morning visit with Meg would ameliorate any hard feelings he may have caused by leaving her without a dancing partner the night before. His guilt hounded him for abandoning her and he had felt wretched the whole evening. According to Kevin, Lawrence's sullen mood brought him nothing but ill luck. The evening ended with Kevin walking away with less currency than what he had brought to the table.

Lawrence took out his calling card when the Deneham's town door opened. He was ready to proffer it to the butler when the servant greeted, “Good day, my lord. You are indeed lucky. The other gentleman had to leave his card for the misses had not yet risen, but she is in the day parlor now. I am sure she will be happy to see you.”

The butler walked off and Lawrence realized he was expected to follow him. He placed his card on the silver salver resting on the foyer's console table as he passed it. He saw Lord Spencer's card. Apparently, Spencer was the "unlucky other gentleman." He removed his beaver hat, gloves, and greatcoat, and handed them with his walking stick to the attending footman. He hurried his actions when he saw the butler had not bothered to wait for him and had to quicken his steps to catch the odd servant before he opened the double parlour doors to announce his arrival.

Lawrence's breath hitched at the tableau that greeted him. Meg was standing next to a circular rosewood table wearing a sprig muslin dress that seemed to match the colors in the large arrangement of flowers that were situated on the center of the table. The light shining through a nearby window created an aura around her graceful figure. He would have been happy to be a silent observer until she acknowledged him if he had not noticed how fixated her eyes were on a piece of paper. His temper rose when he considered the paper captivating her attention might be a *billet-doux*. Without thought, he strode to her side and snatched the love letter from her hand. Lawrence perused the epistle and returned it to her, noting her surprise at his conduct. He checked his anger by biting his bottom lip, before remarking, "It is a Shakespeare Sonnet."

Meg looked back down at the poem, "Yes. I believe it is, though I am not familiar with his work."

"Really?"

Meg blushed. Even though she knew a debutante was not schooled in academics, but in those genteel manners that marked a lady of quality, she was embarrassed she had not read anything of Shakespeare. She enjoyed reading and like other girls her age, she secretly devoured all the gothic mystery and romance novels that were the current rage. Her education had focused on making her a capable hostess, so she never studied books of literary significance. Instead, she learned to become proficient at embroidery, playing the pianoforte, painting with watercolors, and speaking French. Yet, as accomplished as she was, she still felt she needed to apologize for herself, "I fear Mama's library is regrettably thin in the classics and my education is neglected in that area."

Lawrence regretted his remark. He did not mean to suggest Meg's education was deficient and wanted to appease her, but he did not want to find himself in an embarrassing situation when Meg's mother arrived, "I expect Lady Deneham will soon join us."

Lawrence noticed Meg's butler had left the parlour doors open as propriety dictated, but Meg was a maiden, and as such, required a chaperone.

The viscount's inquiry puzzled Meg until she deduced the reasoning behind his question. A grin tugged at her lips, "Normally, Mama would come to greet her guest, but I expect she will think you have come to see me. She will not intrude."

Lawrence frowned, "Does she not sit as chaperone when you have male suitors?"

"You are far from a suitor." Meg wished she had not revealed her thought. The truth was she wished his lordship was courting her for she liked him very well, "If someone visited whom Mama thought questionable, you can be sure she would be attending me."

Lawrence grinned at the silent compliment and took the sonnet from her hands. He placed his palm under her elbow and escorted her over to the sofa, guiding her to sit, then sat next to her, "I would feel honored if you would allow me to introduce you to Shakespeare's works. I once acted as a tutor. My grandmother and mother, you know, ran a school for young boys."

Meg's eyes gleamed at Lawrence's confession, "I did not know that of you, my lord. I would feel quite honored if you would instruct me. I admit, I feel ignorant to know nothing of his works."

"Nonsense, you are not the only lady not to have studied Shakespeare. I am sure there are many, indeed."

"Will you read it to me?"

Lawrence looked at the sheet of paper, "It is a love sonnet, Miss Deneham. Are you sure you would not rather wait for its sender to exclaim its prose?"

Meg puffed out a rebuke, "Indeed not! I hardly know his lordship and I cannot think of one reason why he would be so bold as to send a *billet-doux* to me!"

Meg's outburst amused Lawrence. He could tell she was angry with herself for showing her temper by the way she fisted and flexed her fingers. Her genuineness moved him and he impulsively placed his hand on hers to comfort her. His touch caused Meg to look into his eyes, "I can think of many reasons why a man would send you a *billet-doux,* Miss Deneham. It seems Lord Spencer can as well, and wishes to court you."

Lawrence's remark stunned her, while she was pleased Lord Atwood thought she could be the object of a man's admiration, she did not want that man to be Lord Spencer. He was too sophisticated for her tastes and she did not trust him. Her instincts told her more than one lady had probably received a copy of the sonnet in her possession, "I am not pleased that on such a short acquaintance Lord Spencer thought it acceptable to send such a bold missive to me. I must admit his lack of decorum makes me quite uneasy. Why, he should not be sending letters to me at all!"

"Indeed!" agreed Lawrence, her charming rant causing him to smile. "And since you have been forthcoming, I will admit I am glad you do not desire his attentions. While I do not like the fact he sent you the sonnet, I am happy I am the one to profit from it. May I read the poem to you, Miss Deneham?"

Meg said she would like it very much.

She watched Lawrence silently read the sonnet as though he was memorizing the words before he returned his attention to her. She looked into his whiskey-colored eyes and listened while he chanted the prose. The cadence of his smooth voice held her captive.

Since I left you, mine eye is in my mind;
And that which governs me to go about
Doth part his function, and is partly blind,
Seems seeing, but effectually is out;
For it no form delivers to the heart
Of bird, of flower, or shape, which it doth latch;
Of his quick objects hath the mind no part,
Nor his own vision holds what it doth catch;
For if it see the rud'st or gentlest sight,
The most sweet-favour or deformed'st creature,
The mountain or the sea, the day or night,
The crow or dove, it shapes them to your feature;
Incapable of more, replete with you,
My most true mind
thus maketh mine eye untrue.

A few seconds passed before Meg realized he had finished the sonnet, "Oh, Lord Atwood, that was beautiful, but what does it mean?"

Lawrence laughed and then chided himself when he saw his chuckle embarrassed Meg, "I am so sorry. I was not laughing at you, only enjoying your genuine appreciation for the sonnet. Remember, it is my responsibility to decipher the prose for you."

Meg raised her head, shook off her embarrassment and with less emotion asked Lawrence again, "What does it mean?"

"Shakespeare likes metaphors. I mentioned this was a love poem. The male lover, in this case, Lord Spencer, is explaining since he left you he is incapable of seeing, of recognizing anything of the outside world because his mind is preoccupied with you. He is blind to his surroundings, no matter what form or figure, he finds your features in them, for all he can see is you."

Meg started to laugh. Her body started to shake as she did her best to quell her giggles. Lawrence found himself affected and started to laugh as well. When they finally gained control of themselves, he asked, "What was the jest, Miss Deneham?"

"I pictured Lord Spencer tripping and bumping into everything in his path because he is unable to see anything but me."

The butler's entrance had them turning to him and they simultaneously rose when they saw a visitor came to call on Meg. Lawrence felt his lips start to quiver at the hilarity of Spencer's arrival. He almost expected the man to trip as he entered the room, not being able to see anything but Meg. The idea was so funny he turned to see if Meg was imagining the same scenario. He had to bite his bottom lip to keep from laughing. The sight of Meg doing the same almost made him lose control of the chuckles he struggled to hold within.

Lord Spencer crossed the threshold into the parlour and halted when he saw Miss Deneham was not alone. Her face was flushed and her eyes gleamed with amusement. He noted her companion was also affected and then, to his chagrin, he saw the gentleman held the sonnet his secretary had scribed on his behalf. He checked his temper. He was miffed a member of the peer was witness to his wooing and wondered how the man came to own the *billet-doux* intended for the lovely Margaret Deneham.

She created quite a picture standing there in a jonquil muslin day dress patterned with some type of flower. He especially liked the low cut of her bodice, but in all honesty he knew her dowry is what charmed him the most. His friend Mr. Grantham mentioned her as a viable prospect for matrimony. Miss Deneham had been through more than one Season and as yet, had not seen success in the *marriage mart*. Apparently, her direct and public manner in expressing her opinions and feelings discouraged her suitors. The *on-dit* was the gentlemen who sought her good opinion did not wish to be saddled with an independent and freethinking woman, no matter how much they enjoyed her company.

Lord Spencer did not care since he was interested in a *marriage of convenience*. The wealth she would bring to the marriage is what mattered most to him. Miss Deneham's superior connections were a bonus. Inconsequential details like her personality did not concern him for he knew a strong word or hand could alter anyone's behavior. Once Miss Deneham became his wife, he had no doubt he would mold her to his liking.

Spencer advanced and took Meg's hand. He was greatly disappointed when she attempted to withdraw it from his grasp. He held firm and quickly brushed his lips on the back of her hand before releasing it. It surprised him to see her clench her hands before exhaling her salutation.

"Good day, Lord Spencer. May I present Lawrence Cowper, Viscount Atwood to you?"

"Your servant, Atwood."

Lawrence smirked and nodded his head in greeting. He held up the notorious sonnet, "I understand you are a lover of Shakespeare. I must thank you for allowing me the opportunity to instruct Miss Deneham on his merits of prose."

Spencer raised an eyebrow and with effort maintained an air of indifference. He looked at Meg, "Did you enjoy the sonnet, Miss Deneham?"

"I am not a study of Shakespeare, my lord, but even though Lord Atwood's instruction was enlightening, I must ask that you desist in sending me such correspondence. It is wholly improper as I am sure you very well know."

Spencer was not pleased to be scolded in front of another gentleman and felt the sooner this young harridan was under his influence the better. He professed his regrets, "I do beg your pardon, Miss Deneham. I am indeed a lover of Shakespeare and the sonnet was a prelude to an invitation to accompany me this evening to the Theatre Royal to see the production of *Shakespeare's A Midsummer's Night Dream*. Edward Kean is performing and I thought you would enjoy it. Please believe me when I say I meant no disrespect in sending you the sonnet."

Meg felt ashamed. Perhaps, she had overreacted. Even so, she was happy to decline the undesirable invitation, "I am sorry, my lord, but I am otherwise engaged this evening."

"I see. Perhaps, you are free tomorrow night. It is their final curtain on this production and I would be most honored if you would give me a chance to offer you my own instructions on the playwright's prose." Spencer smiled at his cleverness. He knew it would be *beyond the pale* for her to refuse again, unless she truly was engaged, which he doubted since she was stumbling for a response.

Lawrence felt Meg shiver while she grasped for a viable reason to refuse the gentleman's offer. He knew she did not wish to accept Spencer's invitation and was earnestly trying to find an excuse. Her sigh revealed her failure and before she felt compelled to accept, Lawrence announced, "I am afraid Spencer that Miss Deneham has already accepted my own invitation to take her to tomorrow's showing. It appears we were on the same quest in our visit today."

Spencer knew he was lying. He had done his research and knew Miss Deneham had no suitors. He had considered himself lucky thinking the lady would be easy to seduce, but with Atwood acting as her protector, he would have to apply himself more diligently, "I hope you own box seats, Atwood, for I am told the play is completely sold out."

Lawrence smirked at the man’s sneering confidence and simply nodded.

Spencer did not like Atwood's grin. It looked as though he was laughing at him. He wanted to tell him he knew he was lying, but held his tongue. He would have the last laugh when the viscount failed to secure theatre tickets. He had told the truth when he said the show was sold out. His satisfaction would come when he expressed his sorrow at not seeing them at the show, so instead of cursing them now, he offered his most charming smile, "I will be sure to pay you my respects during the play’s intermission. While your company, Miss Deneham, is my loss, I am pleased you will not miss out on this most exceptional performance. I will take my leave of you now and call another day when you are not otherwise engaged." Spencer made his bow to her and gave a nod to Lord Atwood before he departed. He left without escort from either the butler or his hostess.

“Do you really have access to a box, my lord?”

“It seems I do. If you will pardon me, Miss Deneham. I will also take my leave of you, so I may secure the details for tomorrow night. I will see you at dinner.”

“I cannot thank you enough, my lord, for coming to my aid. I thought I would have to accept Lord Spencer’s invitation, since my mind failed to produce a plausible excuse.” She paused before admitting, ”There is something in Lord Spencer’s manner that makes me feel ill at ease. It is as if I am being hunted.” Meg shook her head and then added, “I know I am being silly and beg your forgiveness for my foolishness.”

Lawrence took her hand and placed a soft kiss on the inside of her palm. He felt her pulse race and looked into her eyes, “You should always trust your instincts, Meg. They will never fail you.”

Unlike Spencer's touch, Lord Atwood's intimate gesture did not repulse her, so she could honestly respond, "So, it seems."

Lawrence hoped he did not meet anyone he knew while he walked back to Felton's town home. The questions bombarding his mind thoroughly distracted him from his surroundings and most likely from any person who attempted to greet him. Worse, he feared the conversation rattling in his brain would soon vocalize itself. The last thing he needed was to have someone witness his agitated behavior and question his sanity. *What was he thinking involving himself with Miss Deneham? Why should he care whether Spencer has designs on her? And why of all things has he appointed himself her protector? Surely one missed dance did not obligate him to her?*

He could not believe he acted like a feral animal protecting his domain. Whether he liked it or not, he responded to Spencer's interest in Meg as though the man was a rival and that could only mean he cared more for Meg than he thought. Her *joie de vivre* initially brought her to his attention. Even though Meg had a habit of vexing him, he could not deny he admired her genuineness. He liked how she did not employ those manners designed to lure a titled gentleman of fortune into marriage and yet, here he was contemplating marriage.

Lawrence took his walking stick and slammed the tip of it on the ground, releasing a curse. His emotional outburst caused his beaver hat to tilt and he abruptly set it right before continuing on his way. His mind was awhirl with conflict. He argued he was too young to be considering marriage and had at least ten years before the pressure to sire a son to inherit his title would worry him. Unlike a lady who was considered past her prime and unfairly labeled a spinster when she hit five and twenty, a gentleman became more desirable as he aged. While Meg was far from being dubbed a spinster, Lawrence knew like all debutantes, especially ones with more than one Season behind them, Meg would not risk the anathema being applied to her. Her parents would see her settled before her name was bantered about in the parlours. Damn Spencer for setting his sights on her and forcing him to worry!

He wasn't ready to become emotionally entangled, especially to a woman who constantly discombobulated him, nor did he desire to contract a marriage for mutual benefit. He knew what it felt like to live in a home surrounded by love and he would settle for nothing less than a *love match*. Perhaps, that is what bothered him about Spencer. He knew his lordship wanted a *marriage of convenience*. The man required a fortune to support his lavish lifestyle and it galled Lawrence he had targeted Meg to fill his coffers. She deserved better and while he intended to thwart Spencer's plans, he did not mean to usurp them.

He considered it might be best to remove himself to his property after he escorted Meg to the theatre. Time and distance from Meg would clear his head. His cousin was having a birthday party for her daughter and he had promised to attend. He could take Mr. Donahue with him. He knew the American wished to visit his country estate before he journeyed home. Kevin's departure was just a fortnight away. *"Yes,"* he thought, *"I will see if a little distance between me and Meg will cure me of these serious notions. I will speak to Mr. Donahue, but first I have to find tickets for tomorrow's play."* Lawrence hoped Felton owned a box at the Theatre Royal, so his pride would not suffer a setback.

Simmons opened the door to a very wide-eyed and gaping viscount. Unknown to the butler, Lawrence was still distracted with his thoughts when he reached the door of Felton's town home and was not prepared when the door swung open. The action surprised him and he almost lost his footing when he jumped back. The stoic butler, in his usual unaffected voice, apologized for surprising his lordship, "Forgive me, my lord. I thought you wished to enter."

"Yes, of course Simmons. I was *woolgathering*. No doubt making a spectacle of myself staring at Felton's door knocker."

Simmons made no reply as none was expected and waited patiently for his lordship to cross the threshold so that he could close the door behind him. Lawrence absentmindedly removed his beaver hat, gloves, greatcoat, and handed them along with his walking stick to Simmons, "Is his lordship home?"

"Yes, my lord. I believe he is in his study."

Lawrence thanked the man, a habit from his days of being a commoner and walked off to find his mentor and friend, hoping he could once again come to his aid. He was happy to see the tall mahogany doors to the study were open and Edward did not seem to be engrossed with any estate business. The earl's friendly smile beckoned him forward.

"Atwood! This is a surprise. I see you are troubled. Come in and tell me how I can assist you."

"Am I that readable?"

"To me, yes. I have known you well enough these last years to tell when you are worried, but rest assured others would not suspect you are vexed. I expect it is because you do not feel the need to hide your feelings around me. Tell me, what is wrong?"

"I have somehow managed to embroil myself in Miss Deneham's life. I made a morning call on her to make amends for not claiming a dance I had requested of her last night. During the call, Spencer presented himself and asked Miss Deneham to accompany him to the Theatre Royal. I knew she did not wish to accept his invitation and felt compelled to take action as she struggled with an excuse. Without thinking, I jumped in and declared she had already accepted my own invitation to attend. Then, Spencer, with that annoying gloating air he displays, informed me the show is sold out. Please tell me you own a box and I will not be shown the fool I am for acting so rashly."

Edward laughed, making Lawrence frown and rebuke, "I am glad to offer you amusement, Felton."

"Do not take offense, Atwood. While I am amused, I am also sympathetic to your dilemma. I regret to inform you I do not own a box at the Theatre Royal; however, I will attempt to help you. For what show do you need tickets?"

"I am to escort Miss Deneham to tomorrow's final curtain of Shakespeare's *A Midsummer Night's Dream*. Spencer is to visit us during the intermission. I believe he thinks my invitation a ruse and expects not to see us."

"Then you will have to disappoint him, Atwood. Let me see what I can do, but I advise you to confess your folly to Miss Deneham, just in case my efforts prove futile. You dine at the Denehams this evening?"

"Yes."

"Do not look so distressed. I am sure Miss Deneham appreciated you for saving her from Spencer's unwanted attentions. I doubt she cares if she attends the play or not."

"If I am not there, Spencer will feed the clubs with my foolishness and before I know it, the *ton* will be making bets on my courting abilities."

Edward teased, "Are you courting Miss Deneham?"

"Absolutely not! In fact, before I misrepresent myself any further to the Denehams, I have decided to journey to my estate for a few days, taking Mr. Donahue with me. He leaves in just over a fortnight and I know he wished to visit my country home."

"That is kind of you, Atwood, but what about Spencer? Are you not afraid he will press his attentions on Miss Deneham while you are away?"

"She has no interest in him. Besides, her father is more than capable of protecting her from unwanted advances. She does not need me."

His tone serious, Edward advised, "I will tell you word is spreading through the clubs Spencer is in need of funds and he seeks a *marriage of convenience*. I know the ladies find him charming and indeed he can be when he puts his mind to it, but he is also known to be ruthless when he is crossed or when he wants something. He is not one to be trusted, so be chary in your dealings with him." He added, "If you truly do not have any serious intentions towards Miss Deneham, then you are right to remove yourself from her company as not to mislead her."

Lawrence saw Edward's concern and soberly agreed, “I know.” He grimly left to search out Mr. Donahue.

Chapter Seven

The Deneham dinner was a pleasant affair. Sir Marcus and his wife encouraged a relaxed setting, not adhering to those dictates of etiquette requiring conversation with only one's neighbors. Lawrence was delighted to see discussions cross the table in a warm and friendly manner. The room was full of chatter and based by the grins of the footmen who hovered nearby to serve them, the ritual was a common occurrence.

"I understand your visit to our realm is near an end, Mr. Donahue," remarked Sir Marcus.

"Yes. I will finish my time here visiting Atwood's Manor Home."

"Were you able to complete the business that brought you here?"

"I did, though I can hardly accept the credit. Your faithful daughter took care of my sister's needs and Lord Felton's man of business was efficient in acquiring the rest of the items on my family's and friends' list."

"I am glad your trip was successful. Will you return to work on your family's tobacco plantation or do you have other plans for your future?"

"Actually, I have agreed to work for Lord Felton for a percentage in a business venture. He wishes to export goods to America, focusing on those less traded ports where plantation owners and small communities seek the kind of items I purchased. Currently, only the larger cities offer luxuries like silks, porcelain, and furniture. More times than not, the quality is lacking though the price is not. I am tasked to act as Felton's agent in identifying needs and setting up merchants to sell those goods in demand."

"That sounds like a good investment. Is Felton looking for partners?"

Kevin laughed, "I do not know. You would have to inquire yourself."

Lady Deneham interrupted her husband's discourse with Kevin, "Will you visit England again, Mr. Donahue, now that you have a business arrangement with Lord Felton?"

"Yes. I will need to return with the contracts."

"And after that?" asked Meg.

"My father knows my heart is not in working our tobacco plantation. He has agreed to let my sister and her future husband take over the farm when he retires. Like my grandfather, I have always been interested in breeding horses. My future is not set, but I expect if I have my way, then my path will lead me in that direction."

"It is a shame you did not meet my husband's brother Lord Deneham," remarked Lady Deneham. "He is a great breeder of horses."

"Indeed," agreed Sir Marcus. "Since I know you are already engaged to venture north with Lord Atwood, we will make a trip to visit my brother's estate when you return from America."

"That is very kind of you. I would like that very much. I confess I would enjoy seeing more of your fine country."

Meg turned to look at Lawrence, "You are leaving London, my lord?"

Lawrence felt guilty, but he knew his decision to leave Town was the right thing to do. He had no business playing fast and fancy with Miss Deneham's favor and at three and twenty, he had no plans to wed, especially a lady that caused his emotions to swing from one extreme to another. No, he did not think he could live his life feeling cross one moment and in bliss in the other, *Good grief! Am I that happy when I am in Meg's company?*

It seemed both he and Meg were unsettled for he noticed her cheerful manner had also waned after Kevin announced their upcoming departure from London. The quiet scene encouraged Lady Deneham to signal Meg to rise, so they could leave the gentlemen to enjoy their port.

Sir Marcus said to Lawrence, "I know my wife has already thanked you for coming to Meg's aid, but I wish to extend my own appreciation to you as well. I know Meg does not often watch where she is going, but that does not mean she should not receive all due consideration for her station. Meg means the world to me and my wife. We are forever in your debt, Atwood. You may come to me if you are ever in need of assistance."

"Thank you, Sir Marcus, however, your gratitude is unnecessary. Meg was under my protection. I was duty-bound to protect her as I would any lady in my care."

Lawrence's remark surprised Sir Marcus and Meg's father showed it by raising his eyebrows, "Is that so, then you have no romantic interest in my daughter?"

Lawrence stared, mouth agape at Sir Marcus. The silence resonating in his ears like a loud thrum. Before he could voice a sound, Sir Marcus spoke, "You do not need to reply, my lord. I believe I have assessed what I need to know by your lack of speech. I still stand by my offer. If you are ever in need of a favor, you may call on me."

Lawrence wished he was as sure of his feelings for Meg as Sir Marcus. Finally finding his voice, he thanked him.

After a good half hour discussing Felton's export venture, the men joined the women in the parlour. Lawrence was sorry to see Meg's disposition had not improved and cringed thinking how his confession would add to her distress. He was about to introduce the subject of the Theatre Royal when Lady Deneham asked him, "I understand Meg is to accompany you to see *A Midnight Summer's Dream* tomorrow night, my lord. May I ask who is to act as chaperone?"

In all his focus to acquire seats for the theatre, Lawrence failed to work out the details, including that of a chaperone. He looked to Meg for assistance, but quickly determined that avenue was in vain, since she was unaware of his plight. He stumbled to find the right words, until he finally confessed, "I am sorry to admit, Lady Deneham, I acted in haste in inviting your daughter to the theatre. I thought Lord Felton owned a box at the Theatre Royal when I extended the invitation to her. I learned today I was in error; however, he is making inquiries on my behalf to procure tickets. I am not sure if he will be successful and fear I may have to disappoint Miss Deneham by retracting my invitation."

Lady Deneham looked at Meg and saw her mouth tremble. Her daughter was trying not to laugh, but the effort was pointless since she was unable to check her own mirth. To Lawrence's horror, both ladies chuckled gleefully. He did not think it kind of Meg or her mother to find amusement at his distress; especially since it was for Meg's benefit he had made the invitation blunder.

Lady Deneham took a deep breath to calm herself before asking her daughter, "Did you not tell him we own a box at the theatre?"

Meg looked at Lawrence, "I did indeed ask you, my lord, if you had access to a box and you said you did. I did not think it necessary to inform you of our own because I thought it would be ungracious of me to do so, especially since you were so kind to offer yours." Lawrence watched Meg fight to keep her quivering lips from releasing another chuckle. She looked remarkably absurd trying to keep her lips tightly closed and he erupted with laughter at the sight, breaking Meg's weak control over her own mirth.

"It seems you will not have to disappoint my daughter after all, my lord," teased Lady Deneham. "And since you are in need of a chaperone, Sir Marcus and I will avail our services. Do you think Lord and Lady Felton would like to join us? How about you Mr. Donahue?"

Kevin and Sir Marcus watched the comedy of errors from a safe distance, close enough to hear every word, but far enough away not to become embroiled in the drama. While Mr. Donahue found amusement in the scene transpiring before him, he was not inclined to waste an evening at the theatre. He graciously declined her ladyship's offer, knowing he would rather hit the clubs than watch a Shakespearean play. After all, he did not have a young and charming female to tempt him into attending.

Uncomfortable, Lawrence turned from the effusive Lady Felton and looked out the carriage window hoping his disengaging manner would cease Anne's perpetual discourse regarding Meg. He was relieved to see they were making their way down Catherine Street, for if his manner did not dissuade her from talking about keeping company with Meg, then should their arrival at the theatre. They had all agreed last night, since it was more convenient for each household to travel to Covent Garden in their own coach, to meet in the Deneham's box at the Theatre Royal. He would have taken his own coach had he known Lady Felton was going to be excessively chatty about his inviting Meg to the theatre, "It was extremely nice of you to invite Miss Deneham to see the play, Lawrence."

Lord Atwood gave up trying to appear indifferent to her comments and turned back to answer her, "So you have remarked upon more than once, my lady, but one may argue the Denehams invited me, since it is their private seats from which we will be viewing the performance."

"A trivial detail that does nothing to minimize your thoughtfulness."

Lawrence looked to Edward for assistance, but saw only an amused grin. He tried to divert Lady Felton from the subject of Miss Deneham by inquiring of the earl, "Why is it you do not own a box, Felton?"

"The theatre is indeed fashionable and Kean's performances entertaining; however, it is difficult to hear the performers. The large theatre holds over three thousand people. The boxes are too far away from the stage. I have noted if not for the flamboyant scenery and the special effects, the audience would be bored senseless since little of the dialogue is heard, though I admit Kean's baritone travels well. The man is an accomplished performer and I believe it is he alone who draws the crowds." He added, "In all honesty, I have not purchased box seats because I have found when I wish to attend, I can acquire access to someone else's box."

"Yet, you were unable to do so on my account," huffed Lawrence.

"Nonsense. As soon as I learned the Denehams had their own suite and Lady Deneham sat on the Board of Directors, I saw no need to procure them on your behalf."

Surprised, Lawrence asked, "She is on the Board?"

"Indeed, she was instrumental in getting Lord Byron, before he left London, along with his creditors to join a subcommittee focused on legitimizing the theatre's drama. The board wishes the Theatre Royal to become London's cultural center."

"How are they faring?"

"The theatre is struggling financially, even though Kean never fails to draw an audience. I am sure it will survive. It has done so in the past."

Lawrence knew this was the fourth building to grace the site backing up to Drury Lane. For years, the royal theatre struggled with artist conflicts, financial stability, management issues and destruction(two theatres burned to the ground), but the sold-out performances of stellar actors like Edmund Kean and the public's desire for serious and literary plays kept the theatre from closing. Since 1814, Edmund Kean has drawn a full crowd and tonight was no exception.

Lawrence trailed behind Lord and Lady Felton as they made their way to the upper floors of the reserved boxes. He helped Edward protect his *enciente* wife by keeping her safe from the pushes and shoves commonplace in the narrow corridor tunneling through the building. When Lawrence finally entered the Deneham box, he saw the posh and secluded venue had an excellent view of the stage and of the pit, where those of the gentry and scholars sat. He knew the commoners hovered somewhere above him in the gallery.

His inspection halted when Edward stepped aside to allow him to make his salutation. Lawrence bowed to Sir Marcus, Lady Deneham, and then turned to greet Meg. He felt his palms sweat when he saw her eyes alight with pleasure. He worried Meg considered him a suitor, but calmed when he remembered she knew why he had invited her to the theatre. He further reasoned that keeping Meg company was nothing more than the two of them finding themselves at the same musicale.

He greeted her and took some pleasure in seeing she was as anxious as himself. He saw her open and close her hands into fists and thought her palms were likely as perspired as his own. His eyes moved from her hands to her face again and without thought, he allowed himself to thoroughly inspect her. She looked enchanting wearing a high-waist evening gown comprised of Urling's patterned lace over a white satin slip. Long white gloves reached past her elbows to meet puffy sleeves of more white satin and lace. The pearl trim on her sleeves drew his focus to her bodice which was similarly trimmed and the figure filling her dress. By the look on her face, he could tell he was being inspected in return and that Meg liked the way his formal black attire fitted him to perfection.

A slight nudge pushed Lawrence towards the front row seats where he had no choice but to sit next to Meg. Lady Deneham and Lady Felton had taken the seats behind them with the earl and Sir Marcus sitting behind their wives. He wished he sat in the back row with the gentlemen, instead of being on display for the entire world to see. He had no wish for the *gossipmongers* to link his name with Meg, so he focused his eyes on the stage as to appear indifferent to her. He thought he was behaving admirably, having only cast his eyes upon her a couple of times, before the performance totally captured his attention. He was so engaged with the play he nearly jumped out of his seat when Meg tapped him on his arm to get his attention, "Aside from Kean, I cannot hear what they are saying. Can you tell me what is happening?"

It pleased Lawrence to offer his assistance to her. He described the scene before them, "Kean is playing Oberon, King of the Fairies. He is upset with his queen, Titania, because she refuses to give the orphan boy she stole from the Indian King to him. The boy's mortal mother was Titania's friend. Oberon wants the boy for his page, but because the queen pledged to care for him, she refuses her king's request. Oberon will not be denied, so he asks his servant Puck to gather a flower juice that has the power to make someone fall in love with the first person they see after rising from sleep. The potion is so powerful the person's only desire is to please their lover.

Oberon plans to use the drug to take the boy away from Titania and then cure her of her passion with another herb. But first he plots mischief by making sure the first thing she looks at and falls in love with is a hideous animal."

"Without hearing the words, the play is similar to an Italian opera," remarked Meg. "When you do not know the language, you must rely on the *libretto* or someone who knows the performance to translate it for you. Thank you for your explanation. I was having trouble following the story."

Lawrence smiled at her astute analogy and then continued to narrate the play. He was rewarded with a giggle from her when the comedy of errors between the Athenian lovers (Hermia and Lysander) on stage unfolded.

The scarlet stage curtains closed and Lawrence immediately tensed remembering Spencer promised to visit during the intermission. He had seen the gentleman and his smirk in a neighboring box when he took his seat next to Meg in the front row. He wondered if Spencer knew the box belonged to the Denehams and he was technically their guest. He did not trust the man, nor did he care for being his and his friend's subject of discussion. He wondered why Spencer did not graciously accept his *conge* from Meg and leave her alone. A blind man could see she did not wish to further an acquaintance with him.

Everyone rose to stretch their legs. Lawrence saw Anne rub her lower back and Edward frown. He was not surprised to hear his lordship announce, "Atwood, can you find your own way home? I insist on retiring Anne, though she argues she is not weary. Unfortunately for her, my wishes take precedence."

"Of course."

"I will see them to the lobby, Alexandra," informed Sir Marcus to his wife. "Can I bring you back a refreshment?"

Lady Deneham looked to her guests to inquire if they wished anything, "Yes, Marcus. Something for all of us would be nice."

Within seconds, Edward, Anne, and Sir Marcus took their leave. Lady Deneham did not miss a beat in inquiring of Lawrence, "How will you entertain yourself and Mr. Donahue on your estate, my lord?"

"I have promised Mr. Donahue a tour of my properties, an introduction to my neighbors, and then to partake in those gentlemanly pursuits associated with country life: riding, hunting, and fishing. My great-aunt, Baroness Litford, is also hosting a party for her granddaughter for which I promised to attend. Mr. Donahue will want to accompany me for he helped to purchase the sweet filly I am anxious to present to my cousin. Of course we won't leave the area without paying our respects to the Dowager Duchess of Aubry."

"You will be gone a sev'night?" asked Meg.

"At least. We are not bound by any engagements other than to return Mr. Donahue in time to board his ship for America."

Lawrence thought Meg looked disappointed and he wondered if he should alter his plans to appease her. He was struggling with what to do when Spencer and another gentleman entered the box.

"Lady Deneham, Miss Deneham, Atwood," he greeted with a smirk. "I am happy to see you availed yourself of such prominent box seats."

Lawrence cringed awaiting Lady Deneham's retort that the box belonged to her family and that Lord Atwood himself was not the host of their party, but a guest. To his surprise, she revealed nothing other than a slow knowing smile that made his own lips quirk.

Spencer continued, "How are you enjoying the play, Miss Deneham?"

"It is difficult to hear, aside from Kean's dialogue, but the folly of the fairy Puck playing matchmaker on behalf of his King Oberon is amusing. Imagine a flower whose juices placed on unsuspecting sleeping eyes, can induce a love so strong it alters one's own desires."

"In our elevated Society where marriages are arranged for mutual benefit, a love potion would probably be highly desirable," laughed Spencer.

"There are some *love matches*," retorted Meg. "Not all ladies are subject to their father's dictates like our Shakespeare's character Hermia. If she had a father like mine who cares about his daughter's feelings, then she would never have needed to attempt an elopement with Lysander."

Spencer found Miss Deneham's remark childish, though revealing, and realized he would have to either seduce the woman or ruin her if he wanted to wed her. Clearly, Sir Marcus could not be enticed to barter his daughter in a marriage contract.

Sobering, he proclaimed, "Of course, you deserve a man willing to court you, Miss Deneham, and to show you..." Spencer immediately noticed how his pretty words were alarming Meg and halted his speech the moment her eyes widened frightfully. He instinctively covered his mouth with his hand and coughed, then he tried to expunge his gaffe by trying to introduce his friend, "I do not believe you are acquainted with Mr. Grantham."

Lady Deneham was first to answer in an uncommonly curt voice, "I know who you are young man, but since we do not socialize in the same sphere, we have never been introduced."

Her abruptness surprised Lawrence, but he was pleased Meg's mother had no desire for Meg to be introduced to the known rakehell.

Spencer quickly drew his visit to a close not wanting to ruin his own good standing with Lady Deneham, but before leaving, he asked Meg, "Are you to attend the Davenport Masquerade, Miss Deneham?" Before she could answer, he added, "If so, it would do me great honor if you would allow me to escort you."

Lawrence did not like the way the color drained from Meg's face. His instincts flared and he spoke before he realized what he was saying, "Once again, Providence seems to favor me over you, Spencer. You see Miss Deneham has already accepted my own invitation to escort her."

Spencer's hands fisted and closed in anger, but he masked his feelings. Only his tight lips gave evidence of his displeasure, "My loss is great, Atwood." Softening his tone, he asked Meg, "I hope you will save me a waltz in consolation, Miss Deneham?"

With a slight nod, Meg begrudgingly agreed. She watched in horror while Lord Spencer took her hand and brushed the back of it with his wet lips. The act revolted her beyond belief and she wished to wipe her hand against her skirt to remove his saliva, but knew she could not. Her temper rose at the man's audacity. She did not like Lord Spencer. The man frightened her with his boldness. She would need to speak to her father and let him know she had no wish to keep his company or consider his addresses. Her body shivered and her discomfort did not subside until she saw Lord Spencer take his leave.

She heard her mother say with humor, "I see your plans have changed, my lord."

Lady Deneham's words resonated and Lawrence could not believe what a contrary person he had become. *Hadn't he made up his mind to remove himself from Meg's company? Then, how is it he is now escorting her to the Davenport Masquerade?* He bit his bottom lip in frustration, but when he saw Meg grinning, his irritation dissolved and he started chuckling, accepting how hilarious his indecisiveness must appear. His laughter encouraged Meg and her mother to break loose with their own unrestrained amusement. They guffawed and giggled wholeheartedly until they realized they were making a spectacle of themselves. Once calmed, Meg remarked to Lawrence, "It seems I am forever in your debt, my lord."

"Nonsense. I failed to remember I had already accepted Lady Davenport's invitation to her masquerade. I owe you a debt of gratitude for saving me from incurring her ladyship's wrath. She never would have forgiven me for failing to attend her ball. What better way to show my appreciation than to escort you to the affair."

At that moment Sir Marcus returned with a couple of servants carrying refreshments. The curtains parted and they sat to watch the rest of the play in good spirits. They had no idea Spencer had heard their burst of laughter and taken it personally. He swore to himself that he would get even.

Chapter Eight

Lawrence sat at Felton's dining table in the breakfast parlour with a fork full of kippers raised to enter his grinning mouth. He thought it quite amusing Mr. Donahue found the smoked split herring offensive. Kippers have been a morning staple among the English, most likely since man learned to create fire, in spite of their strong smell. The small oily fish is split along the dorsal ridge from tail to head in a butterfly fashion, gutted, salted, and smoked. The delicacy can look quite barbaric to anyone unused to the sight. However, the English enjoy eating the salted and smoked fish prodigiously with their eggs. Lawrence, once he saw his friend cringe, could not help but antagonize him by exaggerating his enjoyment of eating his morning meal.

"Really, Atwood, I enjoy fish as the next man, but not first thing in the morning!"

"You Americans do not know what you are missing," laughed Lawrence. Sobering, he continued, "I really do apologize, Donahue, for canceling our trip to my estate, but I felt compelled once again to come to Miss Deneham's aid."

Lawrence explained what had transpired at the Theatre Royal and how it came about he was escorting Meg to the Davenport Ball, making it impossible for them to leave London.

"One apology is enough, Atwood, and you have more than exceeded it. I really am not surprised by your reaction. Will you never admit Cupid has struck you with his arrow?"

"That is absurd, Donahue. Any gentleman would have come to Miss Deneham's aid. Spencer is a predator. His only interest in Miss Deneham is her dowry and I fear to think what length he will go to secure her hand in matrimony. I do not trust him to be alone with her."

"Is he not a gentleman in Society?"

"Only by birth. He is a rogue, a gambler, and spends more money than he earns. He is a true hedonist. I am told his only concern in life is the fulfillment of his own pleasure."

"What of his duty to his country? Does he take his seat in the House of Lords?"

"Only if he can garner a sum for his vote. He is supposed to be courting Lady Barrett, but he hounds Miss Deneham's heels like a dog after his supper."

"I thought the ladies found him charming?"

"Amazingly they do. He is remarked upon as being fashionable and witty; his company is desired by many ladies. The young debs are so infatuated with him their mamas watch them like a hawk when he is near, while the widows are known to brag of their associations with him. His affairs draw some of the highest wagers in the club books and his name is often whispered among ladies taking their tea."

"Yet, Miss Deneham does not welcome his suit?" pressed Kevin.

"No, she does not! She sees through him for the calculating man he is. Meg has a keen intuition and allows it to guide her. She has no inclinations towards Spencer."

"So, we are not to visit your country home because you are Miss Deneham's escort to the Davenport Ball?"

Lawrence rolled his eyes, frustrated he has to offer his explanation again, "My properties are two to three days ride by coach, depending on how far we push them. No sooner did we arrive then we would have to return to make it back in time to attend the ball."

"What about your cousin's birthday?"

"I have already sent a groomsman to deliver the filly you helped me pick out for her. Her disappointment in my absence will be minor once she sees her new horse."

"Then, what are your plans for today, Atwood? I find myself unoccupied since I had expected to be leaving London with you."

"I am off to Jackson's gym to let off some of my pent-up energy. You are welcome to come if you like."

"I have heard of your Gentleman Jackson. I would very much like to visit his boxing club. My pugilistic skills have served me well, but they were learned from experience and not training. Perhaps I can pick up a trick or two."

"Excellent, Donahue. The great man will not engage you in the ring, but there is always someone looking for a sparring partner. There are only a few who John Jackson will spar, Lord Felton for example, but Mr. Jackson is always around to say a kind or helping word. His impeccable manners are the reason they call him Gentleman Jackson. You can box me if you like, but I warn you I am out for blood. I feel so tightly confined I am ready to crawl out of my skin."

"Why? What eats at you?"

"It is this thing with Miss Deneham. I am having a devil of a time trying to set it right."

Kevin pursued, "What thing is that?"

"Blasted, Donahue! If I knew, I would not be having such a go of it!"

They traveled to Bond Street in Lawrence's plush carriage. Kevin could not keep from remarking, "It is a shame you are not attracted to Miss Deneham. I think you would both suit. She seems to like you and I think she is the genuine article."

"I did not say she was unattractive or disingenuous. All I have ever said is I was not currently interested in marriage. It would not be right of me to pay her any particular attention and thereby mislead her."

"So in a way, Spencer's behavior is more honorable than your own, since he is offering matrimony."

Lawrence narrowed his eyes at Kevin, "There is nothing honorable in a man who presses unwanted advances."

"No, indeed," agreed Mr. Donahue. "But what if the gentleman's attentions were welcomed. Would you be amenable to allowing that man to escort Miss Deneham and keep her company?"

Kevin noted Lawrence's flabbergasted face with amusement. The viscount's mouth gaped open and it was clear his mind was contemplating the scene Kevin just suggested and was having difficulty coming up with an answer.

Gentleman Jackson's gym was abuzz with activity. There were men sparring in several areas marked off with a rope. Some patrons were shadow boxing, while other pugilists were exercising with either a jump rope or hitting a bag hung from the ceiling. Lawrence led Kevin to a changing room and was greeted by the well-mannered owner John Jackson. Lawrence had been introduced to the legend by Lord Felton and felt honored whenever the great man singled him out. He was quick to introduce Mr. Donahue to the boxing champion who promised to offer the American some boxing tips after he saw him spar with a partner.

By the time they both changed their clothes and had an attendant tie up their hands with protective gloves, Lawrence realized he was in a more congenial mood. Kevin noted the change and said in good humor, "You have lost your angst, Atwood. I would not fear for my life if you wish to spar with me."

Lawrence smiled at his friend, but before he could respond, Spencer called out to him. He should not have been surprised to see the gentleman, that of late, had caused him so much grief. Lawrence wished he had remembered the man was a regular client of Jackson's for he was in no mood to see him, much less speak to him.

Spencer challenged, "I believe you owe me satisfaction, Atwood, unless you are afraid to enter the ring with me." His comment drew the curious noblemen within hearing distance and the room began to rumble with talk about a possible fight between two aristocrats. Wagers started to be placed and the chatter pulled more of the curious into the growing crowd of observers. Gentleman Jackson entered the tentative fray. He could feel the tension between Lords Spencer and Atwood and knew this would be no friendly sparring, so he tried to deflect the fight, "My lords, may I recommend sparring partners?"

Spencer huffed. He had no desire to be diverted from a fight he expected would give him great pleasure, so he stated in a clear and loud voice, "I have challenged Viscount Atwood, but he has yet to reply."

Lawrence raised his eyebrows in mock surprise, "You are too generous, Spencer. I would not have thought you valued your face so little."

His retort generated a few guffaws from the audience rapidly thickening around them. Lawrence waited to see if Spencer would pick up the gauntlet he threw and settle their conflict with words, but it was not to happen. The gentleman gritted his teeth and angrily demanded, "Well, Atwood?"

Lawrence nodded his acceptance, but not before saying, "I hope you have no pressing engagements, Spencer, for I expect you will have to remain in seclusion until the swelling on your face subsides."

Spencer checked himself from engaging in a verbal battle. He knew he was minutes away from teaching the insolent viscount a lesson, so he held his tongue. With a wave of his hand, he directed Atwood to an unoccupied boxing ring and allowed Lawrence to precede him into the sparring arena. John Jackson followed both men into the ring and then checked the ties on each of their padded gloves before he reviewed the club rules, the same rules the champion Jack Broughton instigated in his own club after he delivered a fatal blow in a 1743 bout.

"All right, my lords, remember no hitting below the belt; no hitting once your opponent is down or on his knees; and only wrestling holds above the waist are allowed."

Atwood and Spencer took their position, bending their knees, tucking their chin into their chest and bringing up their fists to protect their faces. They carefully took each other's measure and then they slowly circled, looking for an opening to strike. Spencer, confident in his ability, was the first to jab with his right. He was older, had more weight on him and a longer arm span than his opponent. His smirk revealed his contempt for the viscount and when his fist connected with Lawrence's face, he smugly turned to his cheering supporters to accept their accolades.

Lawrence felt the sting of Spencer's fist on his cheekbone and became momentarily disoriented. He fought to regain his equilibrium before Spencer could assault him again and did his best to shake off the burning pain from Spencer's decisive hit. He immediately took a defensive stance and was surprised to see Spencer disengaged from their bout, distracted by the roaring crowd. It was an amateur's mistake to take his eyes off his opponent and Lawrence took full advantage of it. While Spencer accepted his congratulatory praises, Lawrence bent low, swung his fist and undercut Spencer's jaw with enough force to throw him off balance. He pressed his advantage and pelted the man's face until he heard him cry "enough." Lawrence could see he had drawn blood and realized if he had not heard Spencer's shout of misery, he most likely would have continued pummeling him. Feeling guilty, Lawrence backed off of him and watched while John Jackson came to Spencer's aid. The room quieted. Everyone appeared frozen in place, shocked at the outcome. They waited to see what damage the viscount caused and while they waited, Lawrence left the ring to change his clothes. Kevin followed him, "Are you well, Atwood?"

"You should be asking Spencer."

Lawrence was not happy he lost control of his temper, letting his rage overcome him, "I should have stopped before I damaged his face, Donahue. The match was for sport not vengeance."

"Spencer suggested differently."

"Not really, it was all for show. If Spencer truly wanted vengeance, he would have sought me out privately, where gossip could not tarnish his charming reputation."

"Well, I don't know about his reputation, but I expect your fight with him today will draw you into the spotlight again. Why don't you head to Lord Felton's town home and I will wait around to see what damage you have done to Spencer's face. You should probably apply a beef steak to your own cheek before the bruising sets in."

"Thank you, Donahue. I'll see you later then." He quickly changed his clothes and without a look over his shoulder left the gym.

Lawrence was happy when Simmons announced Lady Felton and the earl were presently not at home. He was impressed Felton's butler was able to keep a stoic resolve after seeing his undoubtedly bruised and swollen cheekbone. He was having trouble remaining aloof under the butler's scrutiny, his cheek feeling the daggers of pain when he grimaced under the man's inspection. It was clear

Simmons was curious, but the old retainer was too dignified to ask how he sustained his injuries, "May I recommend a beef steak and a soothing balm, my lord?"

Much to Lawrence's chagrin, he smiled at the butler's consideration and quickly felt a multitude of sharp pricks assault his cheekbone again. He exhaled an anathema while with the pressure of his hand he tried to soothe his throbbing bruise, "Yes, please, and have a bath prepared for me. I shall retire until supper and Simmons, I am not home to callers."

"Very good, my lord." Before attending to his lordship's command, Simmons picked up a package on a nearby console table and handed it to Lawrence, "This came for you earlier, my lord. A Deneham footman delivered it."

Lawrence took the box and climbed the staircase, making his way to his private suite of rooms. He placed the bounded box on his bed and then sat in a nearby chair to await his valet, Feebes, knowing Simmons would have passed on his order for a bath to be made ready for him. He slouched into his chair to await his servant, stretched out his legs before him and closed his eyes to rest. His head fell back on the chair frame and he exhaled deeply. He could not believe the rage that had overcome him when he saw Spencer smirk at him. It was that same contemptible grin he offered Meg each time he was in her company. The one making her feel afraid and the one that distracted him enough to allow Spencer to connect with his cheekbone.

He knew Spencer's gloating foolishly opened up the opportunity for him to deliver a substantial blow to the man's chin. In hindsight, he should have stopped fighting then, but in that moment, he was so emotionally charged he did not even realize the fierceness of his attack until Spencer called out.

"What a fiasco," thought Lawrence. *"The ton will have a field day with it. The only saving grace is those near enough to hear Spencer's challenge would have nothing other than conjecture to determine why the man demanded satisfaction."*

Lawrence's head was beginning to pound. He pulled the bell cord to hasten his valet and thought the man a genius when he entered a moment later carrying a tray holding a snifter of brandy.

"You read my mind, Feebes."

"It is in my best interests to do so, my lord." Feebes handed the liquid elixir to his master unable to keep his twitching smile at bay, "I do hope your opponent's face is worse than yours."

"You are impertinent, Feebes. But you may rest assured you have no need to hide your head in shame. I believe I prevailed better than my opponent."

"Very good, my lord." Feebes watched his master tip the short-stemmed glass of brandy until the liquor was uncommonly swallowed in one long gulp, then turned to arrange his master's ablutions, "I will have your bath ready in a moment, my lord."

Lawrence stood before the full-length cheval glass mirror and saw for himself how improved he was after taking a relaxing bath and repose. Unable to sleep, he had used the time to reflect on his actions. He wanted to make sure he learned from his errant behavior for he did not want to be a man who let his temper override his reason. Spencer had purposely provoked him and instead of ignoring him like a mature man, he let his emotions engage him in a fight like a schoolboy being taunted. Felton would never have let anyone goad him into doing something jejune. The earl always seemed to move and make decisions in a deliberate manner and Lawrence thought that was a wise approach worthy of mirroring. He cringed and regretted grimacing the moment the pulsing burn crossed his cheek. He touched his bruised cheekbone and realized how lucky he was that Spencer was a vain fool, looking at his cheering audience rather than his opponent. Otherwise, he would be the one licking his wounds this evening.

He continued his inspection of himself until he was satisfied with his valet's administrations. Then, he praised, "Feebes, you have out done yourself again." The valet was about to give a second brushing to his coat when Lawrence spied the package he had chucked earlier from his bed. It lay haphazardly on a nearby chair and he remembered how Simmons said a Deneham footman delivered it. He impatiently waved off Feebes and went over to open the box. He placed it on the bed, untied the twisted yarn binding the top to the bottom and tentatively removed the lid, unsure of what he would find. He was surprised of its contents. A note written in a fine delicate hand rested on top of the garment. It read:

My Lord Atwood,

Do forgive my lack of propriety in sending you this note. Rest assured it is no billet-doux, but only a word from one friend to another. I hope you allow me to call you friend for you have been very kind to come to my aid on more than one occasion, therefore, I cannot but regard you highly.

I have taken the liberty to send you Lysander's costume for the masquerade ball. I took advantage of Mama's connection with the theatre and since the play ended its run, I was able to secure both Hermia's and Lysander's wardrobe. I thought it would be amusing to wear them and knew you would appreciate the mischief.

I can understand if you would prefer another attire. After all, you are not a suitor and may be uncomfortable, even in costume, to connect yourself with me. I do hope I have not offended.

In friendship,
Miss Margaret Deneham

Meg's inane way of being both conniving and honest amused Lawrence. He knew he should not wear the costume, but he would anyway. He did not want to disappoint her and for the life of him he could not understand why.

He replaced the lid to the garment box and put the package on top of his walnut tallboy. He had just turned around when he heard a knock sound at his door. He beckoned, "Come" and saw his valet enter. Lawrence was surprised to see his servant return so soon. He raised an eyebrow at him, "Well, Feebes?"

"I was asked to summon you to his lordship's study. You have a guest waiting and the earl is entertaining him until you arrive."

"Do you know who it is?"

"No, my lord."

Lawrence rechecked his image in his mirror again before making his way to Felton's study. He paused at the threshold, surprised to see Sir Marcus Deneham in what appeared to be a most serious discussion with the earl. The mood was somber and Lawrence felt the hairs on the back of his neck prickle when he entered the room. He could tell something was amiss and felt it in Edward's greeting, "Atwood, I shall leave you to your visit." The earl bowed his head to Sir Marcus and departed.

"Sir Marcus," greeted Lawrence. "This is a surprise, but indeed a pleasant one."

Sir Marcus did not smile and Lawrence became anxious wondering what caused a man of good humor to be so fraught and angry. It did not take long for him to discover, for like his wife and daughter, Sir Marcus was a thoroughly direct and honest person.

“Atwood," he ranted. "It did not take long for the fight between you and Spencer to reach the clubs. I was enjoying a winning set of cards when your melee was narrated and the cause of the fight conjectured. My daughter’s name was mentioned and is already being wagered upon at this minute as one of the women behind your disagreement. I will not have it! I have already visited Spencer and berated him for the imbroglio. I informed him his addresses for my daughter are not welcomed and he will no longer be received into my home. I am here to tell you that you will be refused as well.”

Lawrence was dumbstruck. He did not expect to be affronted in such a manner, “I do not understand your ire at me, Sir Marcus. Have I not always been a friend to your daughter and shown her only the highest regard?”

“Yes,” he replied begrudgingly. “But, you know as I do you have no serious intentions toward Meg, even though your actions suggest otherwise. Now this fiasco with Spencer has her name bantered about as though she needs saving from an unknown disgrace.” He bellowed again, “I will not have it!”

“Miss Deneham’s name was never mentioned,” gritted Lawrence. “Spencer and I were simply sparring.”

“The *ton* will not accept such a *taradiddle*. There is no known connection between you and Spencer other than my daughter. The *on-dit* is spreading like water bursting through a fractured dam: rapid, powerful, and destructive. By tomorrow, my daughter’s name will be tossed about in every tearoom and her virtue questioned. I will not add to the fodder by allowing either you or Spencer to compete for her hand and make her a spectacle." Sir Marcus gave a mock laugh, "Compete indeed, for you have no desire to win her hand, do you, Atwood?"

Lawrence did not know how to respond. He felt foolish when he could only think of Meg's sorrow, "Then, you would have me disappoint your daughter and not escort her to the Davenport Masquerade Ball?"

"I fear you have already disappointed her in withholding your addresses. I have supported Meg's wish to have a voice in her betrothal and have not intervened when she has refuted eligible offers. She is desirous of a *love match* and since Providence presented me with such a gift, I found I could not refuse her, but mind you, she is not lacking. She is not without admirers, nor does she need you to escort her. She has a bevy of gentleman eager to make a connection with her and I have chosen one who has faithfully loved her, who has waited patiently for her to accept his addresses. She will not miss your absence, Atwood. You are herewith released from any obligations you may have made to her." Sir Marcus abruptly turned and left without another word. Lawrence's mouth gaped open. He was still staring with his jaw dropped at the empty threshold when Lord Felton entered.

"I am sorry, Atwood. I know you are not to blame. I am sure Spencer provoked you."

"Thank you, Felton, but the fault is mine. I should not have let my pride spur me into fighting. Can you imagine anything more childish than to engage in fisticuffs because someone suggested I feared them?"

"It is a challenge that cannot go unanswered. You would have been abjured by your peers if you did not engage. The *ton* loathes a coward. Your err was in the amount of damage you did to your opponent when you were just supposed to be sparring."

"I see your point, Felton and must admit I am not sorry to have thrashed Spencer, but I do regret I embroiled the good name of Miss Deneham."

"Is that all you regret, Atwood?"

Lawrence frowned, "What do you mean?"

"Will you not miss the company of Miss Deneham? Sir Marcus informed me your society would no longer be welcomed."

Atwood did not answer. Felton looked over his friend's confused demeanor, sighed, and before making his exit, offered, "I suppose this incident has solved your problem with Miss Deneham. You no longer need to worry about your intentions being misconstrued since her company is now denied to you."

Lawrence had trouble grasping that he could no longer call on Meg. He was so absorbed with his thoughts, he did not notice the earl's departure. All he saw was his conversation with Sir Marcus. The scene playing over and over again in his mind. He kept trying, without any success, to determine if he could have managed a better outcome for himself if he had responded differently. He could not believe he was not welcome in the Deneham home and when he fully accepted the idea, his whole being disheartened. He felt as though he was thrown from his horse, out of breath and bruised. The realization his conduct was the reason why he could no longer call on Meg made him angry, causing him to bark at Mr. Donahue when his friend entered the room. He bitterly asked, "Where the deuce have you been?"

Lawrence's outburst surprised Kevin, "What burr is under your saddle, Atwood? You are the one who refused visitors or have you forgotten your instructions to Simmons?"

"I am sorry, Donahue, but I am having a rough day. First, this imbroglio with Spencer and then Sir Marcus informed me I am *persona non grata* with his family. My good humor is spent and I am not the best of company."

"Well, perhaps knowing the result of your fists will keep Spencer away from Miss Deneham and other young misses for a good week, if not more, will improve your temperament. You did not break his nose, for that he is grateful, but his battered nose and cut lip are swollen. Plus, when I left his two eyes were already turning shades of purple. He is not fit to be seen. I expect he will hold up in his residence until the swelling and bruising subsides."

Kevin added, "To save his pride, he is blaming his vanity for his injuries and telling anyone who cares to listen he gifted you the opening that allowed you your victory. He says he most likely would have murdered you, if his attention had not been diverted from the fight."

"That man has no sense of discretion, Donahue. Will he make this into a greater scandal than it is already?"

"I did not know it was a scandal, Atwood."

"The *gossipmongers* are spreading the tale faster than the ground covered by England's best thoroughbred at Newmarket. I have just been seriously rebuked by Sir Marcus." The weight of his words caused him to drop his head and groan as the consequences of his actions fully hit him. He found Kevin looking at him with concern when he finally raised his head, "He has forbidden me to call on Miss Deneham."

"Ah," exhaled Kevin. "Now I understand why you are so forlorn and not rejoicing over Spencer's defeat. I am truly sorry, Atwood. I know how much you favor Miss Deneham."

"I do?"

Kevin knew the question was rhetorical and did not bother to answer, "Come, I am sure Lord and Lady Felton await us in the parlour."

Chapter Nine

Meg sighed. She looked at the shepherdess reflected in the giltwood mirror hanging on the wall of her private suite of rooms and exhaled another long breath. Her less than enthusiastic reflection made her remember how much she wanted to enter the ballroom with Lawrence as a couple, her in Hermia's gown and Lawrence wearing Lysander's costume, but without a Lysander as escort, she was uncomfortable presenting herself as Hermia. Therefore, she felt extremely lucky, though sorrowful, to have found another ensemble to wear to the masquerade ball. At least she could feel happy her parents never knew about the costumes she acquired from the Theatre Royal. They would have been mortified to learn she acted so boldly and she would have been embarrassed to see her parents pity her for admiring a man who did not return her esteem. She knew they were as disappointed as herself when they discovered Lord Atwood had no desire to court her.

It seemed longer than six days her father had summoned her to his study to inform her of the gossip that she was embroiled. She remembered being frightened when she entered his private office to find him uncommonly pacing and exhaling expletives. She could not remember a time when he had lost his temper, at least, not in her presence. His hair was amiss with errant hairs sticking out suggesting he ran his fingers through it a number of times. His cravat was loose and crumpled. Always immaculately dressed, it disturbed her to see him in complete disarray.

Clearly troubled, Meg rushed to his side. She was surprised to learn a fist fight between Lords Atwood and Spencer was at the root of his distress. More importantly, was the gossip naming her as the lady behind the melee. Meg knew Lawrence boxed, but she never considered him dangerous. He was not a violent man. He was more a prince in her mind than a brute, but her father thought differently. He told her she was no longer free to receive either gentleman. She did not mind Lord Spencer being denied access to her, but the thought of not seeing Lawrence saddened her, so she tried to reason with her father, arguing that Lord Atwood was not a physical threat to her. When her father finally agreed, Meg thought he would relent and allow her to receive him, but Sir Marcus was adamant, claiming any connection with his lordship further risked her reputation, "Even now the *ton* sits waiting to see how this drama will play out. They will be watching you, Spencer, and Atwood, waiting for a tiny morsel of innuendo to fuel their tales."

Unfortunately for the *haute ton,* the subjects of their gossip withdrew from the spotlight. Viscount Atwood left London and Lord Spencer secluded himself at home to nurse his wounds.

Meg continued to look at her reflection in the mirror while she struggled with the concept of how a person could be alone in their remarked feelings and then she thought of Simon, whose admiration had never wavered. She remembered how he surprised her at her debut ball by passionately confessing he loved her and while she loved him in return, it was not in the way of a lover. Sadly, knowing her feelings did not equate to his own, she refused his addresses.

She had known Simon Ware since she was a child and held nothing but fond memories of him. He was kind, generous, and he accepted all her vagaries, never taking offense when she spoke her mind or laughed with feeling. He always looked at her with affection and never once did he show any sign her exuberant behavior embarrassed him. They got along splendidly and she treasured their friendship. Each year, he religiously offered for her hand in marriage on the anniversary of her debut into society and each time Meg refused him. She wanted Simon to find someone who could return his passionate feelings and she wanted someone who stirred her own emotions.

Meg wanted to marry for the type of love where one's heart swelled in anticipation of the other. She had never known that kind of excitement until she met Viscount Atwood. At times, her stomach churned with such nervousness, she thought she would be ill. Other times, she was so happy the world around her was a blur, nothing seemed to hold her attention, but him. She knew this was the type of love Shakespeare explored in his sonnets, where the most mundane activities brought joy, simply because the activity was shared with a loved one, whether it be in mind or body. Meg loved spending time with Lawrence and when she was not in his company, she liked thinking about him, wondering what he was doing and what it would be like when they met again. Most of all, she wondered of his touch, his kiss, and his embrace. She wished more than anything he would satisfy her curiosity and take her into his arms for she did not know if she was simply infatuated with Lawrence or if her heart was truly engaged.

In her youth, her adventuress spirit allowed more than one young man to steal a kiss from her, but those moments had always been awkward and embarrassing. One admirer closed his eyes too soon and ended up kissing her nose; another young enthusiast banged his teeth with her own. She quickly lost her curiosity about kisses and decided when she made her debut she would be more discriminative about who she encouraged to keep her company. Her hopes had been to find a witty, charming, gallant gentleman who stirred her emotions.

She was beginning to believe no one would ever interest her and then she met Viscount Atwood.

"It is karma," she thought. *"My punishment for not returning Simon's ardent love."* She sighed again, realizing her father would never allow a union between Lawrence and herself even if the viscount wished to pay his addresses to her.

Meg descended the staircase and saw Simon waiting with her parents in the foyer. He was dressed as her shepherd and smiling at her with his faithful devotion. She knew she loved him too much to saddle him with a dispassionate wife. Life would be a lot simpler if she could return his feelings, for Simon's love was something that never failed her. It amazed her how he was always close by when she needed him.

"You look quite enchanting, Meg."

"Thank you, Simon. You look very rural yourself and I am grateful for your escort of me this evening."

"It is always my pleasure to accompany you, Meg." Simon took the stole from the butler, placed it on Meg's shoulders and without further ado left for the Davenport Ball.

Meg's father had been serious when he said the Deneham household would not receive Lord Atwood, so when Lawrence began to heatedly complain about Sir

Marcus's unfair decree, Edward thought it was time to remove the young viscount from London before he did something rash. He suggested a trip to visit his great-uncle, the Marquis of Beaumont, reminding Lawrence that Kevin would enjoy the visit since he missed seeing the Atwood home.

Beaumont Manor was only an hour away from London on horseback and less than two by carriage, depending on how fast one traveled, and Edward felt the journey was more than manageable for his, heavy with child, wife. They all left the morning of the Davenport Ball. Lawrence and Kevin led the journey on fresh mounts with Edward and Anne following in their stately coach at a slower rate. The young men traveled side by side at a gentle canter, avoiding the ruts and potholes of the highly used lane. They checked their pace, making sure they did not venture too far ahead of Felton's carriage. The silence between them nagged at Kevin until he was the first to speak, "For a man who complained of being entangled with Miss Deneham, you do not seem relieved of the severed connection."

"I never complained of Meg's company, Donahue."

"My ears must have been impaired then, for I was sure on more than one occasion you complained she annoyed you and you feared your attentions might be misconstrued."

The quiet pause hung like a curtain while Kevin waited for a retort to his recollection. He surmised his friend was shielding his feelings, not only from him but from himself. Since the beginning, Kevin thought the chemistry between Lawrence and Meg was palpable. So much energy pulsed between the two of them it was hard to miss, either showing itself with sweet affection and sparkling laughter or cutting tension and emotional outbursts. Only a fool would miss the attraction between them and Kevin did not believe his lordship a fool.

"I may have misjudged the situation," stated Lawrence under a hiss of breath.

"Well, what do you plan to do about it?"

"What can I do? Sir Marcus refused to see me. I tried to ameliorate the situation by presenting myself to him the day after his visit. I had hopes I could convince him to rescind his ruling that keeps me from calling on Meg, but I could not make it past his butler. The impudent servant would not even take my card!"

"You British are a nation of proprieties. Why not simply elope with Miss Deneham? I am sure she would be willing."

"Then you do not know her very well, Donahue. She would not dishonor her parents in such a way. Besides, if we were to become betrothed, it would be with an honorable offer and courtship."

"You are incredulous, Atwood! Do you still not know your own heart?"

"What do you mean?"

"You said 'IF'!"

Lawrence was glad the marquis dined early compared to London hours where dinner was never presented before eight o'clock. He was not sure how he managed to contribute to the table conversation, but he was glad when everyone seemed eager to end the evening. The Marquis of Beaumont was at an august age where he retired to his bed early. Anne was exhausted after the day's journey and took her husband to their suite immediately following the end of their meal. Even Mr. Donahue seemed to know Lawrence wanted to be left alone, for he departed to the billiards room without offering an invitation to his friend to join him.

Lawrence wrestled with his thoughts as he made his way to his private suite of rooms. He waved off his valet and plopped himself into a wingback chair facing the fireplace. The fire had been recently stoked and Lawrence watched the white hot flames flicker, his mind struggling to place a name on the feelings he held for Meg. He recalled Mr. Donahue's retort, *"Do you still not know your own heart?"* Perhaps, he did not. His own father was a merchant marine who had died at sea when he was a young boy. His mother never remarried and while he did not remember the love his parents shared, he did recall the melancholy descending on his mother when she thought of her absent husband. If love was sorrowful, then he must be in love, for he was not feeling too cheerful at the moment. His thoughts were challenged by a dose of reasoning when he recalled how happy Lords Felton and Westfield were in their marriages. Any discontent they experienced came when they were not able to please their wives. *Was his displeasure drawn from knowing he disappointed Meg? Did that mean he loved her? How did one know when they were in love?* Lawrence knew he was attracted to Meg and enjoyed her company. He also accepted she could rile him to distraction. He acknowledged on more than one occasion he placed himself as her protector. *"But,"* he argued, *"any gentleman would do the same, or would they? And how would he feel if they did? Would he relinquish that precious role to them without a care?"*

Agitated, Lawrence rose and grabbed the fireplace poker to jab at the burning logs. He watched the flaming embers spark and crackle before he returned the utility to its stand. Then, he walked over to his side console table to pour a snifter of brandy Feebes had set up for him. The brandy reminded him how he had retired his valet for the evening and would have to singularly ready himself for bed. The recollection made him cringe knowing he would have a dickens of a time removing his tailored coat from his shoulders. The current fashion had a gentleman's jacket fitting so tight it felt like a second skin. He took a sip of his brandy before walking over to set the balloon glass down on his bedside table. He took the nearby seat to remove his boots and immediately jumped out of his chair when he felt and heard the crackling sound of an object being crushed. He cursed Feebes for the incident, but his temper subsided when he recognized the box containing Lysander's clothes.

He had intended to return the costume to Meg this morning, then changed his mind when he realized it was his last connection to her. He thought as long as he possessed the article, then he had a reason to approach her again, even if only by a courier. Lawrence remembered how he insisted his valet pack and bring the box with them to Beaumont's.

Lawrence lifted the lid and ran his hand over the smooth velveteen of Lysander's cloak. He started thinking about the Davenport Ball and how much Meg wanted for them to attend as a couple. Before he even realized he was plotting, an idea began to take shape. He laughed, knowing he should not follow through on his scheme, but knew he would anyway.

The Davenport Ball was a crush. The ballroom was filled to capacity with members of the *ton* dressed as fairies, queens, peacocks, pirates, sultans, and knights. The less flamboyant and faint of heart wore the standard domino and half mask. From the street, onlookers saw a grand town home exploding with bright lights and heard garrulous chatter from every opened window. Carriages were lined in a row along the sidewalk farther than one could see with their coachmen working their team to bring their master to the front door. It was after midnight and members of the *ton* were still arriving.

Meg stood next to Simon and her parents in the ballroom. She just finished a set of dances with her escort and found her mouth parched. She wished with all her heart Lawrence was in attendance, but even with his absence, she was halfheartedly enjoying herself. Simon was good company and he never failed to raise her spirits. She chatted and laughed her way through their dance and now begged him to collect some lemonade to quench her thirst. Sir Marcus decided to accompany Simon and collect a drink for his wife. Within seconds, Meg was alone with her mother. She was admiring the authentic looking costume of Mark Anthony and his Cleopatra when she was distracted by a masked man coming into her view and gasped.

The man greeted her mother with a bow and then turned to her, "May I have the honor of this dance, Miss Deneham?"

Meg nearly shrieked when she saw Lysander standing before her. While his half mask and cap disguised his facial features, she recognized him immediately and feared the Shakespearean costume would blatantly identify him to her mother. Meg thought he looked splendid wearing an exquisite velveteen cloak over an elaborately embroidered doublet and jerkin. His short wide breeches were puffed out with padding and his muscular legs were covered in netherstock hosing. He made a striking gentleman of the Elizabethan era. Meg even noticed his shoes were adorned with rosettes. She smiled, knowing he had dressed to perfection to please her.

Lysander proffered his arm and Meg looked to her mother for permission. She did not wish to disobey her father, but hoped her mother would grant her this favor to enjoy Lord Atwood's company one last time. Lady Deneham narrowed her eyes. She flattened her mouth in disapproval showing Meg she knew the identity of her masked gentleman. Meg was about to refuse Lawrence when her mother exclaimed, “I am quite able to entertain myself, Meg. I suggest you accept this gentleman’s offer before your papa returns.”

Meg laughed and joyfully thanked her mother. She quickly placed her hand on Lawrence’s arm and allowed him to lead her unto the dance floor. She was so happy to hear the melody of a waltz she almost hopped with glee. The intimate dance would allow her a more congenial setting to talk to Lawrence. She desperately wanted to ask him why he came, especially knowing she was forbidden to receive him. Since their initial meeting, it seemed she had been nothing but trouble for him. She ached to know why he bothered with her at all; especially when he claimed he had no desire to court her.

“Why are you here, Lysander?”

"To find Hermia of course.”

“But I am not Hermia.”

“You are incognito, but Hermia nonetheless. You make a fetching shepherdess; though, I disapprove of your shepherd.”

“Simon is all that is good and wanting in a suitor. I am lucky he chooses me above all others."

"Does he?"

"Does he what?"

"Choose you?"

"He has honorably asked for my hand in marriage on more than one occasion."

"You have refused him?"

Meg frowned and asked again, "Why are you here, my lord?"

"I did not want to disappoint you."

"But why?" demanded Meg.

Lawrence saw the hurt in her eyes when he did not answer. It wasn't that he did not want to answer her, just that when he opened his mouth to speak, he found he had lost his voice.

Simon and Sir Marcus frowned simultaneously when they returned with their refreshments and saw Meg was missing. Lady Deneham nodded her head in the direction of where her daughter danced with a masked man and had to elbow her husband in the rib when he started to shout in anger.

"If that impudent puppy thinks he can ignore my dictates, he is in for a rude awakening!" Sir Marcus was about to stride over and snatch his daughter right out of the viscount's hands when his wife whispered, "Let Simon do it."

Meg looked unhappy and Simon wondered what the masked man said to cause her such grief. He was not alarmed for her safety since he could easily protect her, but he was concerned her feelings had been hurt. Meg had a keen sensibility and though she tried to act indifferent when she was criticized for her less than coy manner, he knew the masked man's remarks affected her deeply. Simon instinctively strode across the ballroom floor to break up Meg's and Lawrence's dance.

"Excuse me, Meg. Your mother wishes to take her leave."

Meg looked from Simon to Lawrence and feared her heightened emotion would choke her from expressing her courtesy as manners dictated. She felt a modicum of relief when she heard her own voice, "Thank you for the dance, my lord. I bid you good evening." She quickly curtsied, grateful she had not uttered a word of dispair, and allowed Simon to lead her off the dance floor.

"Who was that man, Meg?"

"Only a character in a play."

Simon was used to Meg's conundrums. It was her way of shielding her heart when it was in danger of being hurt, "Is he an important character, Meg?"

"Not anymore, Simon. I fear I misjudged him and must now pay the price for my foolishness."

"Will it cost you much, Meg?"

Meg pulled on Simon's arm and dragged him through one of the French doors lining the Davenport Ballroom. She led him onto the terraced balcony where she was happy to see they were alone. She placed herself in front of Simon, so she could look into his eyes. He was a caring and affectionate soul and she wished he could make her heart flutter, "Simon, why is it, even though you have professed your love on more than one occasion to me, you have never tried to kiss me?!"

"That is not true."

"The year of my fourteenth birthday does not count!"

"Do you remember what you told me after I took your lips by surprise?"

Simon knew through the change in Meg's eyes and the giggle floating from her mouth she remembered, "I told you if you ever did that again without an invitation, I would cease to be your friend."

"Your friendship is too dear to me to risk it in such a fashion."

"I am inviting you now, Simon. Will you kiss me?"

"Why?"

"Because I fear I may have erred in my feelings for you."

"And if you have not?"

"Then I will still love you and remain your dearest friend as before."

Simon gripped Meg's arms and brought her closer. He raised her chin to see her face. Her eyes were open and pleading. He could tell she wanted their kiss to mean something and he hoped she felt as much passion as he knew he would feel when their lips joined. He cupped her face with his hands and brought his lips to hers. He saw her eyes flutter close and her lips begin to softly pucker before he kissed her. He was concerned someone might intrude upon them, so he only pressed his lips softly onto hers. He was about to release her when he realized Meg's arms had not embraced him. They hung by her side as though she was waiting for him to finish. If he was to be judged by this one kiss, then he would engage her with every bit of experience he owned. When he finally released her lips, he noticed how Meg was holding on to his shoulders for support and could not keep from grinning at seeing her lips delightfully swollen from his ravishment. He looked into her eyes, expecting to see them dazed in wonder. While he may have kissed her to distraction, he knew from what he saw that he had failed to win her heart.

Meg opened her eyes, grinning, "You are most talented, Simon. I can tell you have not pined away for me these past years. I do hope you haven't broken too many hearts in your endeavors."

Simon laughed, "You are incorrigible, Meg. Am I to surmise your heart is immune to my attentions?"

"I will never be unaffected when it comes to you, Simon. You own a piece of my heart, though I will admit another gentleman, an unworthy one at that, possesses the remainder. If it is any consolation, I know what it feels like to love someone remarkably and not have those emotions returned."

"He is a fool, Meg."

"As am I Simon, for not loving you as I should."

"We do not choose love, Meg. It chooses us. Come, let us find your parents before our disappearance becomes fodder for the *gossipmongers*."

Chapter Ten

It was nearly one o'clock in the afternoon before Lawrence opened his eyes to a darkened room. From his tester bed he could see Feebes left the curtains drawn, so the morning light would not precipitately awaken him. He threw back his counterpane, thinking to rise, then abandoned the idea and fell back onto his feather down mattress, dropping his arm across his eyes, surrendering his weary body and soul. All night, he tossed and turned, tormented over the images of Meg in another gentleman's arms. Even now, he could not believe she allowed another man to touch her, much less kiss her.

Lawrence did not mean to follow Meg and her shepherd out onto the terrace. He felt wretched knowing his silence caused the sorrow he witnessed in Meg's eyes and without thought, he trailed behind the pastoral couple when they turned and took their leave of him to make sure Meg was all right. It surprised him when Meg pulled Simon onto the terrace instead of returning to her family and then his shock turned into desolation. Sadly, he watched Simon draw a very willing Meg into his arms.

All night he wondered why his voice left him when Meg pressed him for answers. He was not a green boy. He bantered with young and experienced ladies of the *ton* and never once did he fail to produce a retort. She had asked, "*Why did you come?*" His response was easy to voice, *"Because I did not want to disappoint you."* And then she had to confound the moment by asking, *"Why?"* again. He wanted to tell her he knew it would make her happy if he came dressed as Lysander, but the inadequate words stuck in his dry mouth. He had yet to put a name to what he felt for Meg and before he could offer a response to her inquiry, Simon had taken her away. He watched them leave and like a floundering fish, struggled in duress with his mouth gaping, until his worry over Meg compelled him to close his mouth and follow them. Nothing surprised him more than to see Meg drag Simon onto the terrace.

It took every ounce of his control not to pull Meg out of Simon's arms. He had to walk away lest he intervene, especially when he saw Meg was engaging in the kiss and had no need of a rescuer. He traveled directly to Beaumont's without changing his clothes and gave the ostlers a nice chuckle when they saw a glimpse of his attire under his greatcoat.

Two hours passed from when he first opened his eyes before Feebes outfitted him in proper attire and fed him a repast to assuage his overwhelming hunger. Ready to greet what was left of the day, he went in search of Mr. Donahue. Simmons told him Kevin was at the home farm where Beaumont had sheep shorn and produce grown for his household.

Still feeling a little ragged after his late night, Lawrence decided to ride his horse over the circuitous route to the farm rather than take the lengthy walk through the grove to get there. He could hear the baying of the sheep when he neared the property and the memory of his first sheep-shearing contest assailed him.

He remembered how Beaumont, after naming his great-nephew Edward his heir, was eager for him to marry and beget a son to continue his line. No sooner had the Prince Regent, through a letter of writ, bestowed one of Beaumont's lesser titles on Edward, proclaiming him the Earl of Felton, than Beaumont hosted a ball to gather eligible ladies for Edward to find a wife. He had resurrected the Sheep-shearing Festival, as a form of amusement, for those guests sojourning through the week preceding the ball. Lawrence remembered it was the vexing Lady Anne who won Edward's heart. His pursuit of her was not an easy one, since the lady distrusted his rakish reputation, but Edward persisted and eventually prevailed when Anne accepted his marriage proposal. It pleased Lawrence the happy couple would soon be able to present Beaumont with the heir that secured the title for another generation.

Lawrence spied Kevin tightening his mount's bridle near the main stables. He was glad he caught up to him, for it looked like he was ready to take his leave, "What do you think of Beaumont's home farm?"

Kevin placed his foot in his stirrup and mounted his horse before replying, "Looks very well-managed. I am told your tenants are in the process of bathing their sheep so they can bring them here for their bi-annual shearing."

"Yes, indeed. Clean wool brings a better price. Felton acts as selling agent for himself and the local farmers. As a member of the peerage, he can negotiate a fairer price for the sheared wool than a commoner could on his own. No one would think to cheat a lord, especially one with Felton's business savvy. I must ask him if he will host the Sheep-shearing Festival. You will be sorry to miss it, if they do host the affair. I would think you would like to try your hand at shearing."

"Shear a sheep?"

"Precisely, it is quite challenging. I have much respect for the shearers. It takes great strength to restrain the sheep and then to shear its wool into long pelts. The shearers are amazingly fast, especially considering the number of sheep they have to shear. They are well-deserving of the festival Felton holds in their honor."

"I will be very sorry to miss the event. Tell me, Atwood, Have you sheared any sheep?"

"Only in the festival contest where a few sheep were left unshorn for the event. I teamed with Felton. As novices we were allowed to partner. I held; he sheared. It was hard work and I am more than happy to leave it to the experts."

Kevin laughed, "You are getting soft in your elevated sphere, Atwood. Come on, let's put these horses to their paces. You have beautiful country and I want to enjoy as much of it as I can."

"You should have seen him take the hedgerows, Felton," remarked Lawrence at dinner. "He is a natural horseman. He could easily showcase any hunter needing selling."

Edward raised a brow to Mr. Donahue and found him embarrassed over Atwood's accolades.

"I have always enjoyed riding, my lord."

"Years ago," interjected the Marquis of Beaumont who was listening intently to Lawrence's enthusiastic praise, "when I was a boy, my father would host a hunt on our properties. It was a wonder to see all the magnificent horses take the field. Some of the steeds were eighteen hands tall. The pageantry of the riders in their crimson coats, gleaming black boots, and top hats were quite a remarkable sight to a boy of eight."

"Have you ever hosted a hunt yourself, uncle?"

"No, Edward. While I like to ride, I never took pleasure in watching the hounds slaughter a cornered fox."

Edward heard his wife gag and turned to see her cover her mouth with her table linen. Beaumont quickly apologized, "Forgive me, Anne, for my thoughtlessness."

"Nonsense, my lord. It is only being *enceinte* that causes me to be highly sensitive. You are not to blame."

"Regardless," intervened Edward with sympathy. "We have plenty of other dinner topics we can discuss. I understand, Mr. Donahue, you visited our home farm. How did you find it?"

"Impeccable, my lord. Your steward should be applauded for his management. I understand you are gathering your sheep to be sheared."

"Indeed, it is that time of the year."

"Will you host the festival, Felton?" asked Lawrence.

"I thought I would skip it this year, though I will host the banquet for our tenants and laborers. I would be remiss not to do so."

"You did not speak of this to me, Edward," remarked his wife.

"Or me," added Beaumont.

Edward reached for his wine goblet, took a sip of the rich burgundy and dabbed his lips with his *serviette* before he answered. He looked pointedly at his wife who looked quite put out, "I thought in your condition, it would be better to skip the festivities this year. I do not wish to tax you, my lady wife."

"I am no invalid, Edward. Besides, your man of business sees to everything. I simply nod my approval here and there. Do you mean to deny me this pleasure?"

Edward laughed, "I cannot be so easily cajoled Anne. You do more than nod your approvals. You know very well our home will become invaded with company if we host our festival. I have already received inquiries from many of our friends showing their interest to attend. I will not put you and our baby at risk by burdening you with a house full of guests."

Anne held her tongue and took a calming breath, holding her husband's eyes with her own, "We will speak of this in private, my lord."

"As you wish," smiled Edward.

A busy schedule of entertaining Kevin with daily rides and touring the countryside helped Lawrence to forget Meg for a time, but then his mind would conjure images of her in the quiet evening hours. He was in constant agitation over why he had trouble declaring himself to her. *Was he afraid of commitment?* He knew he did not fear affection, for his mother and grandmother had showered him with it. *Was he simply scared of taking on the responsibility for another human being? Could he be that shallow?* No, he knew that was not the reason, but he did know he was exercising extreme caution and the more he thought about it, he realized Meg scared him. Not her exactly, but what he felt for her. *"Is it healthy to be so captivated with another human being?"*

Having Meg's company denied to him was proving more difficult than he ever imagined. Not only did he miss her company, but he was becoming agitated thinking about the liberties the shepherd was taking in his absence. *"What if Meg accepts the shepherd's offer of marriage before he could decide what he wanted to do?"*

He became even more distressed when Lady Felton shared her correspondence regarding the *on dits* of the *bon ton.* A day did not pass when some tidbit was written to her regarding Meg's newfound popularity among the noble elite. Lord Spencer was once again paying Meg particular attention to the annoyance of her constant escort Simon Ware. An offer from either of the gentlemen was being widely speculated.

"It seems she is highly sought-after," Anne commented. "Alexandra writes your own gallantry in Cheapside on her daughter's behalf is still remarked upon, though she is happy to report your imbroglio with Lord Spencer seems to be forgotten."

Lawrence's temper rose at the news, "How is it Spencer is permitted to keep her company. Were not both of us banned from her society?"

Anne softly reminded Lawrence, "Lord Spencer is astute enough to understand a *cut* from a highly connected family, like the Denehams, will hurt his standing in the *ton.* I am sure he was patient before humbling himself before Sir Marcus. A remarked and earnest apology to Sir Marcus and his family was probably atonement enough for his cavalier pursuit of Miss Deneham. I doubt very much he seeks Meg out in private."

"Then, may I expect the same consideration?" asked Lawrence.

His query perked everyone's attention and they waited while the countess checked her temper. She looked pointedly at Lawrence, "Have you made amends to him or his family for your duplicitous attentions towards Miss Deneham?"

Lady Felton's reprimand shocked Lawrence and like a boy who was caught feeding the mutt at the dinner table, he slouched into his chair and hoped to become invisible. He knew the question was rhetorical. Everyone knew he had done nothing to explain to Sir Marcus or Miss Deneham his confounding behavior regarding Meg. If anything, he angered the patriarch by showing up at Sir Marcus's home the day after he became *persona non-grata.*

Anne took pity on him, "Alexandra did not remark upon it, but I am sure we will find out soon enough. The Denehams have accepted our invitation to sojourn with us during our festival."

Lawrence searched out Edward who simply lifted his shoulders in acknowledgement. Anne saw her husband shrug and laughed, "Did his lordship not inform you, Lawrence? We will indeed host our festival and ball this year."

"Do not gloat, Anne," remarked Edward. "It is most ungenerous of you."

"Forgive me, my lord. You misinterpret my felicity for gloating. I am most appreciative that you have reconsidered to host our festival. I am the happiest of wives."

Beaumont knew the amorous play between his nephew and his wife could take on a life of its own, so he put a stop to it by inquiring, "I understand you take your leave of us in two days, Mr. Donahue. I will be sad to see you gone and even more sorry you will miss our festival."

"As am I, my lord. I cannot thank you all enough for your kindness and hospitality. I am looking forward to my business venture with Lord Felton and hope it strengthens rather than diminishes our bonds of friendship. Commerce does have a way of creating a chasm among associates."

"Nonsense," stated Edward. "I am too levelheaded and magnanimous to risk a respected friendship in business. Our goodwill to one another is safe, Mr. Donahue. I look forward to your return. I expect you will spend the Little Season and Christmas as our guest."

"As you wish, my lord."

Distressed, Anne asked, "Are you seeing to Mr. Donahue's departure, Edward?"

"I would not leave you to see to our guests alone, Anne. However, Atwood and my man of business, will be absent to accompany Mr. Donahue."

Startled, Anne looked to Lawrence, "But what of Meg?"

"Have you forgotten I am forbidden to approach her? It is best I am not here to cause her discomfort. Did you not say she is expected to accept Mr. Ware's offer?"

Anne held her tongue. She wanted to shake the foolishness out of Lawrence, but she was not at liberty to reveal what she knew. Only she was privy to Alexandra's remark of how disappointed Meg was Lawrence had not paid his addresses to her. Both ladies hoped a forced encounter between the young couple would reconcile their feelings, with Meg and Lawrence either admitting their true feelings for each other or accepting they indeed did not suit. It seemed, with Lawrence's absence, the best-laid plan would not come to fruition and Anne was becoming irritated she had changed her husband's mind to host the festival. Edward was correct in assuming she had no wish to host a household of guests while heavy with child. She had no one to blame but herself for the impending task and considered it her due punishment for meddling in other people's affairs.

Lawrence stood on the landing dock, inhaling the briny sea air, sorry to bid adieu to Kevin. He reluctantly proffered his hand, knowing the handshake would be the catalyst that sent his friend to board his ship. He felt his throat constrict when he confessed, "I am sorry to see you go, Donahue. I have gotten quite used to your company."

"I am glad to call you friend, Atwood. You are a good man, though a foolish one. I hope you do not live to regret your action or lack thereof, regarding Miss Deneham."

"Give leave, Donahue. You have done nothing but rail at me since we left Beaumont's."

"As only a friend can do. Take care of yourself, Atwood. With God's Will, I shall see you in three months."

"My best regards to your family, Donahue. God speed."

Lawrence left the docks. He did not wait to see the ship sail into the horizon. He felt restless and when he entered his carriage, he commanded his driver to take him to his club. He had stayed awake through the evening talking with Kevin until the wee hours of the morning. Kevin could have boarded the ship the night before and taken to his cabin to sleep, but Lawrence was happy he preferred his company to a well-rested night. There would be plenty of time for Kevin to sleep on his journey. Lawrence would miss his American friend and he decided to take his soberness to White's for a quiet repose. He thought spending time at his private club would serve him better than making his way back to Beaumont's, where his feelings for Miss Deneham would once again be provoked.

Guests were already arriving at Beaumont Manor the day Lawrence and Kevin left for London. It took three days for Kevin to settle his affairs and inspect his inventory. Felton's man of business was exceptional, but Kevin liked to make his own final check of his cargo.

Lawrence was glad to spend the time with him even if it was in the hole of the ship counting and examining the man's crates. Lawrence even tolerated Kevin's harping on him about Meg. Now that he was gone, he found himself revisiting Kevin's reasons why he thought he and Meg belonged together. He cursed, wondering what the deuce was wrong with him that he did not realize before now he loved her.

He entered the lounge at White's and began to make his way to a corner table when he spied Sir Marcus at another table sitting alone, drinking a cup of coffee while reading *The London Times*. Lawrence knew if he approached Sir Marcus and the man gave him the *cut direct* the affront would plague him for years. The speculation from his peers over the cause of the insult would mar his reputation and probably place him on the fringes of the *bon ton*. It was only seconds, but it seemed a lifetime of indecisions passed, before he realized it was time for him to act. If he truly loved Meg, than any risk was well worth enduring to win her hand in marriage. With his shoulders back, he approached Sir Marcus and made his salutation.

Sir Marcus must of sensed being observed for he dropped the newspaper and raised his eyes to find Lawrence frozen in place. Meg's father made no attempt to acknowledge the viscount or *cut* him, he simply raised his brows in inquiry.

"I bid you good day, Sir Marcus and ask for a moment of your time."

"As you wish."

Lawrence let out the breath he was holding and became hopeful, "May I join you and send the footman to have your cup refilled?"

"You may desist with the pleasantries, Atwood. Speak your peace before I lose my patience with you."

"I would like to apologize, sir."

"For what?"

Lawrence took the seat opposite Sir Marcus and explained, "It was thoughtless of me to engage in a bout with Spencer where your daughter's name could be bantered about."

After an excruciating pause, Sir Marcus finished his coffee. Lawrence looked on as Meg's father fastidiously dabbed his mouth with his table linen, folded it, then placed the napkin on the table. It was obvious with the man's face coloring crimson and his lips tightly sealed that he was doing his best to hold his temper. Sir Marcus pushed out his chair to rise and Lawrence instinctively rose in unison. An overwhelming wave of panic hit him when he heard Sir Marcus say, "If that is all you have to offer, you have wasted my time, as well as your own."

Frantic, feeling that his only chance of securing Meg was slipping through his grasp, he ardently confessed, "That is not all, sir. I deeply regret I did not know my own heart, I hurt your daughter and in turn, my own aspirations for a happy future. Please forgive me for the lovesick fool I am and allow me to pay my addresses to Meg."

Sir Marcus, surprised by the young man's sincere declaration, sat himself back down in his chair and commanded Lawrence to sit as well, "You think you know your heart do you? Then tell me, when Meg gets embroiled in a topic peaking her interest, how will you feel when you hear her garrulous voice resounding throughout the room?"

"I will be glad she is happy and enjoying herself."

Sir Marcus prodded, "How about when those animated hands of her makes contact with something or someone?"

"I will always stand by her, Sir Marcus. Her welfare and happiness are my greatest priorities."

"Are you sure, Atwood? Many have failed her. She is her mother's daughter and I personally find her exuberance charming. How do you know you will not take offence over her natural disposition?"

Lawrence smiled and did not hesitate to explain, "I find Meg most attractive in all things."

"Then, perhaps, you are worthy of her," replied Sir Marcus who found the viscount's smile comforting. It was as if the man was envisioning Meg. "The choice is hers, Atwood, but I must warn you, your reluctance to declare yourself cut her to the core. I do not know whether she will give you the time of day. I fear your window of opportunity to win her hand in marriage may have passed."

"As long as you welcome my suit, Sir Marcus, all is not lost. Tell me, why are you not at Beaumont's enjoying the festival?"

"I did not feel right accepting the invitation when I refused my own door to you. It is well known Felton considers you family."

"Then, your daughter is in Town?"

"Heavens, no! I would not refuse them from accepting Felton's hospitality."

"Then I must be off, Sir Marcus. I have a ball to attend and would enjoy your company in my carriage, should you wish to join your family."

"You are quite the strategist, Atwood. Do you think being seen in my company will help your cause?"

"I do not know, sir, but surely it could not hurt."

Chapter Eleven

Meg's eardrums throbbed from the cacophony of chuckles, guffaws and bellows resounding from Beaumont's ballroom. She wished as she neared the festival celebration she could cup her hands over her ears to diminish the painfully loud volume. Unfortunately, such an act would draw remarks from onlookers and she had no wish to ever be a topic for speculation again. She paused at the room's threshold, taking a moment to acclimate to the noise, get her bearings, and search out a friendly face among the motley and boisterous crowd. It was a rare sight to see commoners dressed in their Sunday best clothes mingling with the aristocracy attired in their rich garments. Usually the lower classes were snubbed by their betters, but the festival's sheep-shearing contest encouraged the tenants to engage in conversation with them. Praises like "Good show!" and "Remarkable skill!" were bellowed in earnest. Meg heard only one "Bloody hell!" though she was sure there were others exclaimed.

The festival opened early in the morning with the sheep-shearing contest in the home farm's large barn. The Earl of Felton offered his guests an abundance of food laid out on long tables made out of wooden planks resting on barrels covered with white linen. Footmen wearing the Beaumont livery and housemaids in crisp black and white uniforms diligently worked to keep serving trays replenished with food and drink. Lord Felton also provided a variety of entertainments for his guests to enjoy. He had his man of business schedule a myriad of games throughout the day. Men participated in pie-eating and tug-of-war contests, women entered their jams and pies for best category awards and children entered the three-legged race and sheep-chasing contests. Plenty of booths were constructed to show off the local talents of master craftsmen and weavers. The home-woven woolen textile displays reminded everyone how the art of weaving had diminished now the realm had moved into the industrial age with the use of looms.

Simon's departure from London to return to his family's country home for a few days had disappointed Meg, even though he had promised to return and finish the Season with her. He had been her saving grace the past fortnight while she battled with her emotions concerning Lord Atwood. Even now, she cringed at her foolishness to believe that someone as refined and sought-after as Viscount Atwood would wish to pay his addresses to her. She had left the Davenport Ball feeling wretched, eventually consoling herself that it was not unreasonable to believe Lord Atwood held a true affection for her, since he had a habit of coming to her rescue. After all, no one had forced him to seek her out, nor had anyone coerced him to dress up as Lysander, especially to his own peril from her father. She might have chalked up his behavior at the Davenport Ball to nerves if the man had not left London without leaving her a note of explanation. His lack of consideration was infuriating, never mind the fact the butler was instructed to turn him away at the door. She was more than confident the viscount was smart enough to plot some way to see her. His departure from London inferred he did not harbor any remote feelings for her and she had simply misconstrued his attentions. The revelation was depressing, overwhelming her with a melancholy that shadowed her at every event she attended thereafter. The *gossipmongers* noted her subdued manner and chatted about her newfound refinement. They saw Simon's unwavering adoration and proclaimed Meg had outshone every other debutante in both looks and manner. The accolades drew admirers to her side and before long, Meg was besieged by suitors earnestly trying to win her favor. Only Simon understood she was impervious to their attentions. He knew she was nursing a broken heart and he feared no one, not even himself, had the means to mend it.

Meg saw her cousin, the Honorable Alicia Deneham, beckon her from across the ballroom and made her way to join her. Alicia accompanied Meg and her mother to attend Beaumont's festival and unlike Meg, was enjoying herself immensely, flitting from one group of friends to another. Meg knew Alicia maintained and fostered her friendships with her peers even though she balked at attending the Season. She was not one who favored shopping and making house calls, so she rarely visited London. Instead, she cultivated her relationships by sojourning at her friend's country estates, preferring a bucolic lifestyle to engaging in Town society. She became mistress of Deneham Manor when, at five and ten years of age, her mother passed away from influenza. She adored her father and shared his interests. Baron Deneham, bred and sold quality horses. He was a indulgent parent who did not check his daughter's curiosity at a young age in animal husbandry. If anything, he marveled at her acumen and riding proficiency. Alicia shared her father's love of horses and took great pride that he allowed her to assist him in his breeding farm. Lord Deneham was Sir Marcus's elder brother who inherited his title from their father while Sir Marcus was knighted for services rendered to his king.

"Meg!" called Alicia. "Come join us." Alicia tentatively smiled at her uncharacteristically out of sorts cousin, but then she cheered when she saw Meg's eyes alight with joy at seeing Lord Hathaway, the man with whom she was currently engaged in conversation and ready to introduce.

Meg laughed at the animated lordship and greeted him with felicities. She said to Alicia, “His lordship and I are already acquainted.”

“You need not stand on ceremony with me, Meg,” stated Lord Hathaway. “Though I will revert to decorum and call you Miss Deneham should anyone else join us.”

“You are all that is proper, Miles. Tell me, what were you two discussing? You seemed quite excited before I broke your discourse.”

“Indeed I was, am plum excited, I am. I put on a great show with my two new black bays and I think I might get an invitation from the Four-in-Hand Club. Be quite a coup for me. I would be immensely pleased to wear one of those dandy blue and yellow striped waistcoats.”

“Miles purchased his cattle from us, Meg," explained Alicia. "It will be a great advertisement for our breeding stock if our bays get Miles entree into the *ton’s* premier horse club. Only the best whips are asked to join.”

Miles grinned at Alicia's circuitous praise. Meg watched and listened while the two of them continued their banter regarding horseflesh. Bored, she scanned the ballroom to find something of interest to entertain her, until her companions began a topic for which she could participate. She gasped when she saw her father walking towards her with Lord Atwood at his side. She could not believe they were smiling and that, she found was insupportable. After all the misery she suffered, they had the gall to present themselves as though nothing of significance had transpired. She waited for her father to explain himself.

Sir Marcus asked, "Meg, where is your mother?"

"I do not precisely know, Papa, but probably keeping company with Lady Felton. I did not expect to see you here."

"Nor I imagine did you expect to see me with Lord Atwood. Needless to say, all is forgiven. You may make your salutations to his lordship, for he is once again in good standing with the Denehams and he has my blessing to call on you. I am off to see your mother."

Before leaving, he greeted his niece and Lord Hathaway and then made his way to locate his wife. Meg was glad Alicia and Miles were so engrossed in their conversation they probably missed her father's declaration. She was seething her father and Lord Atwood made amends without her involvement. She wanted to rail at Lawrence, declaim he was far from owning her good favor and wipe the cheeky smile off his face with a hard slap. Her mind was awash with questions trying to grasp the meaning of his reemergence. She was working to calm her agitation when Lawrence asked her to dance. She was too angry to engage him in words or in dance, so she instinctively refused his invitation, informing him she was not inclined to dance. She thanked him and mentally applauded herself for maintaining her manners. She then turned to join Alicia and Miles in their relentless conversation on horses and smiled, knowing she had just discreetly *cut* his lordship by turning her back to him.

Shocked. No other word could describe how Lawrence felt. He could not believe his Meg could be so unforgiving as to *cut* him. If it was anyone else who had dismissed him in such a heartless way, he would have simply taken his leave without care or thought, but he was not about to relinquish his pursuit of Meg so easily. He understood why she was angry with him. After all, he had injured her by not proclaiming himself. If she wanted to be chary then he would be patient, but more importantly, he would be clever. Instead of taking his leave of Meg, he stepped into her circle of conversation, maneuvering himself to stand at her shoulder and offered a smile to the company she kept. Alicia and Lord Hathaway looked at their intruder and returned his smile with felicity. Lawrence had to bite his bottom lip to keep from chuckling when he saw Meg's jaw drop at finding him by her side, no doubt, annoyed he had ignored her rejection. He could tell only her good manners kept her from ranting at him, especially when Miles offered a solicitous greeting.

"Atwood! Wondered where you were. Thought I would see you in this morning's contest. Have you given up sheep-shearing?"

"This year, yes."

Alicia elbowed Miles. "Oh, I do beg your pardon. May I present the Honorable Alicia Deneham, her father, Baron Deneham is an exceptional breeder of fine horseflesh. I own two delightfully fast black bays from his stock. Miss Deneham, I present Lawrence Cowper, Viscount Atwood to you."

Lawrence made his bow, "It is a pleasure to meet you, Miss Deneham. Are you related to Miss Margaret Deneham, per chance?"

"Cousins, my lord. Our papas are brothers and I must admit very similar in temperament. We are highly indulged."

Lawrence kept from grinning, especially when Meg cast a frown at her cousin. He wondered if Meg's cousin could help him and decided to arrange an opportunity to ask her, "Your cousin is not inclined to dance, Miss Deneham. Are you of the same persuasion?"

"Indeed not, my lord." After a moment when his lordship did not proffer his arm in escort, Alicia asked, "By chance, are you collecting scientific data, my lord, on who is or not inclined to dance?"

Lawrence laughed, "Not at all, Miss Deneham, I am hoping you will do me the honor of dancing the next set with me."

Meg scrunched up her eyebrows and Lawrence had to check himself from bursting with chuckles at seeing Meg discomfited because he was to dance with her cousin. It pleased him to see she was not as indifferent towards him as she acted. He heard the string quartet begin to play a waltz and was glad he would have an opportunity to chat privately with Meg's cousin. He hoped they were friends and Alicia would be able to help him court Meg. He proffered his arm to Alicia and escorted her onto the dance floor.

After a few glides around the ballroom, Lawrence complimented, "You dance well, Miss Deneham."

"And you are very charming, my lord. Perhaps, mischievous as well. I must confess I overheard my uncle's remarks. Tell me, are you the reason for Meg's subdued personality? Should I despise you for affecting her so wretchedly, or is all truly forgiven as my uncle declared?"

"You are very perceptive, Miss Deneham, and like your cousin, quite forthcoming with your observations. I am sorry to hear your cousin has suffered for my ambivalent behavior, but I have come to my senses and intend to stay the course until she forgives and welcomes my suit."

Startled, Alicia inquired, "You wish to pay your addresses to my cousin, my lord?"

"It is my heart's desire, Miss Deneham, to make your cousin my wife."

"I had no idea Meg had any true suitor other than Simon." Alicia saw his lordship frown, "Forgive me, my lord, but you must know my cousin has had a number of offers since her *come-out*. Aside from Simon, they all covet her large dowry."

"I did not know there were so many offers. I am aware of Simon Ware's interest, of course, for it is currently being remarked upon among the *ton*. Many expect an offer to be made."

"He made his offer three years ago. He is a stalwart suitor, my lord, and waits patiently for her."

"She encourages him to wait?"

"No, my lord, but until she accepts another offer, he remains hopeful."

"Then, I can only hope your cousin holds me in higher esteem than him. Tell me, Miss Deneham, has she spoken of me to you?"

"No, my lord, but in all honesty, this is the first time I have seen my cousin this year. I fear neither of us is very good at corresponding."

"I will not trespass on your connection, Miss Deneham, but I do hope you will communicate my intentions to her. I hope when she is willing, she will let me pay my addresses to her. I fear she currently begrudges me and won't give me the time of day."

"She is a Deneham, my lord. We are a people of strong character and emotion. If you truly wish Meg for your wife, you will have to be relentless in your efforts. No doubt, she will not risk being injured again."

Lawrence swung his partner when they passed a spying Meg. The surprise of his maneuver caused Alicia to laugh heartily and he took great amusement in seeing Meg disturbed by their glee. When Alicia stopped laughing, he asked, "Tell me about Meg's Simon. Have they been acquainted long?"

"Since birth. Their family estates border one another. Simon is her senior by four years and unlike Meg's other suitors, has always appreciated her *joie de vivre*. He has never checked her behavior or been embarrassed by her manner. Meg is very fond of him."

"You do not say *love*, Miss Deneham. Is that because you do not believe in a *love match* or is it that you do not know your cousin's heart?"

"Meg indeed loves Simon, my lord."

Lawrence balked when he heard Alicia say Meg loved Simon. His misstep almost caused him to fall taking Alicia with him, but thankfully, his agility put him and his partner aright. He was quite put out when Alicia started laughing.

"Take care, my lord, and do not fret, for all is not lost. If the love Meg carries for Simon was of a mettle that you like to refer to as a *love match*, then she would have accepted his offer three years ago. No, I believe, her affection for him is like that of a brother and is not an amorous one."

Lawrence almost chuckled. Alicia saw his bemusement and cautioned him, "Do not rejoice yet, my lord, for Meg would choose the camaraderie of Simon over a *marriage of convenience*, so you are not clear of concern. Do not forget Simon's affection is far from filial. He also desires to make Meg his own."

"Will you help me, Miss Deneham?"

"Your desires are of no concern to me, my lord."

Lawrence opened his mouth to protest, but before he could Alicia continued, "However, Meg's happiness is of the utmost importance to me, so I will talk with her. If I believe it is you who holds her heart, than you can count on me to aid you."

"I can ask for no more, Miss Deneham, and I thank you profusely."

The waltz ended and Alicia placed her hand on Lawrence's arm to be escorted back to Meg's side. They both turned to look at each other when they spied Meg's scowl and grinned.

Once Lawrence returned Alicia to Meg's company, he begged his leave of them. The ball marked the end of Lord Felton's house party and Lawrence knew he would need more time with Meg if he was to break through her stubborn disposition. He sought out Felton and then Sir Marcus to see if the Denehams could extend their stay. The Earl and Countess of Felton were more than amenable to host the Denehams for a longer visit. Lady Felton was quite pleased Lawrence had finally realized Meg was his perfect match. Lawrence was sure Sir Marcus would support his stratagem, but he had no idea how Lady Deneham would receive him, so with great caution he approached the couple in the card room where they were part of a foursome playing whist.

"Forgive the intrusion, Sir Marcus, but when it is convenient, might I have a moment of your's and Lady Deneham's time."

"Of course."

Lady Deneham was all ears, but she refused to give any indication. She was a master at showing disinterest, having learned in her youth, that appearing indifferent garnered her more information. The Denehams finished their hand at cards and then excused themselves from the table. Lawrence led them to Lord Felton's study, the one room he was sure would be empty. No one dared to use the earl's personal retreat without his permission. He opened the door with confidence and bid the Denehams to enter, knowing the earl would forgive his transgression.

"This is rather surreptitious, is it not, my lord, for only a moment of our time," queried Lady Deneham.

"Indeed, madam. I must use every advantage, for like our esteemed Wellington, I am resolute to win. I brought you here to confess I love your daughter and to ask your permission to pay my addresses to her, even though at present I know she is reluctant to receive me."

"Do you think we would aid a man who has injured our daughter," berated Lady Deneham.

Sir Marcus laughed, "Desist, lady wife! All is well between the Denehams and this besotted puppy. He was wrong to hurt our Meg, but young men in love are foolish and Meg's happiness is more important to me than wanting to punish his lordship for causing her distress." He turned to Lawrence and chuckled, "Won't give you the time of day, eh?"

"She has a fine temperament, sir."

"What do you need from us?"

"I need time to press my suit, Sir Marcus. I carry on behalf of the Earl and Countess of Felton an invitation to extend your visit."

"So, you have involved them, have you?"

"It seems, Sir Marcus, my friends understand me better than myself. They are pleased I have finally come to my senses and wish me success."

"Then, by all means, we shall stay as long as I believe my daughter's happiness requires you in it."

"Is my opinion not to be considered, Marcus?"

"Do you object, Alexandra?"

"No, but it would be nice to have been consulted, Husband."

To Lawrence's astonishment, Sir Marcus brought his arm around his wife and nudged her to his side, "Are we not one in all things, Alexandra?"

Lady Deneham smiled and then pushed herself away from her husband, "I shall inform the girls we do not leave tomorrow." She gave a mild guffaw and Lawrence could tell they had a loving relationship. He found it charming to note the display of their ardent affection.

Upon locating her niece, Lady Deneham was surprised to learn her daughter feigned a headache and retired to her guest suite. Alicia informed her aunt that while Meg looked irritated, she was far from ill. She speculated she wanted to avoid Lord Atwood's company and found her best avenue to do so was to remove herself completely from his reach. Lady Deneham agreed with her niece's deductions and left her to seek her own amusements, while she returned to the card room to enjoy the rest of her evening. She asked Alicia to inform Meg they were not leaving in the morning because Lord Felton asked them to extend their visit and Sir Marcus agreed.

She thought it wise to have Alicia inform Meg of their plans since she planned on sleeping into the late afternoon and had no wish to deal with a displeased daughter.

Meg tossed and turned all night trying to determine what compelled Lord Atwood to act the way he did towards her and whether or not she should care. She feared she was setting herself up for another disappointment if she allowed him her company again. She knew he could be an attentive and charming man, but she had misread his intentions before and she thought she would most likely do so again. How could she not when she wished for more than an acquaintance with him? She knew if she felt nothing for him, then his indifference would not bother her, but she did have feelings for him and she was sure he knew of them. There was no pleasure in having a man read her emotions so well. It pained her that he played fast and free with her. *He had no wish to court her or did he? Why else would he seek her good favor?* She could not tell what to make of the situation. All she knew was that he chose to stay by her side when she gave him the *cut-direct*. He asked her to dance and offered her a smile. On and on into the early dawn hours her mind struggled to find answers before she finally fell into slumber.

Meg's maid, Mary, helped her to sit up in bed so she could break her fast. Her body felt weary and she wished she was at home in her own room where she could remain secluded and not draw any attention to wanting to be alone. She expected her late awakening had already alarmed her parents, making them push out their departure time. She knew she could not linger over her morning meal and delay them further. Her exhausted state made her impatient and irritated. She spied her cousin bounce into her bedroom with a cheery countenance which only further annoyed her. Without thought, she brusquely took the cup of hot chocolate Mary proffered her, causing the heated brew to slosh over the cup's rim. Mary offered up an earnest apology for her clumsiness which Meg assured her maid was unnecessary, claiming the fault was her own. Alicia laughed. Meg scowled at her cousin and then gave her a well-deserved scrutiny. She thought Alicia looked much too energetic, especially to someone who had little sleep. She wanted to blame Alicia for the mishap, but knew it would be unfair. Her ill temper began to diminish when the sweet aroma of her rich cocoa reached her senses. She wanted nothing more than to ignore her cousin and sip the delicious brew, but her good manners prevailed. She settled on warming her hands around her cup, while she greeted her enthusiastic guest.

"Good morning, Cousin. Am I keeping my family from departing?"

"Heavens, no! I just became concerned when I heard you were still abed. You are not ill, Meg?"

"No, not at all. Just weary and looking forward to returning home. When does my mama wish to depart?"

"Not today."

"What do you mean?!"

"Lord Felton invited your parents to stay and they agreed. I was informed last night after you retired."

Meg slouched down, almost spilling her cup of cocoa that had yet to pass her lips. Maybe she was ill after all, for she felt her stomach turn over like a wave hitting the sandy shore.

Chapter Twelve

Meg bit her bottom lip in frustration to keep herself from shouting at the servant who, even by late afternoon, could not be persuaded to open the door so she could enter her mother's suite. She turned in exasperation and marched down the hall, aggravated beyond belief, that her mother left strict instructions with her abigail, that on no grounds was she to be disturbed, particularly to Meg's surprise, by her own daughter. Even after three separate attempts, Meg could not get past her mother's steadfast maid. She was a trustworthy gatekeeper, indifferent to Meg's pleas and reprimands, no doubt, one of the reasons why Lady Deneham employed her. Obviously, her mother knew she wanted to rant about their extended sojourn. She could not believe her mother would make her stay in a place where Viscount Atwood was also in residence. With no recourse, she went to expound her grievances to her father, only to learn he was out riding with Lord Felton.

Anxious, with pent-up energy, she strode through the hallways until she ended up in the long gallery.

She noticed right away the Beaumonts were a handsome lot. There was a family portrait of the current marquis when he was a boy in short pants. He stood next to his mother who was sitting on a giltwood chair with his baby sister sitting on her lap. His father towered behind them. The wall was filled with portraits of past generations and of sporting pursuits. One painting showed the marquis's father dressed in his scarlet red hunting jacket standing next to his horse and hounds, while another portrait painted the current Marquis of Beaumont in his library holding a book. Each painting spoke of the family's interests. She took her time to admire each portrait and all the small trinkets and miniatures adorning the marble tabletops of the giltwood consoles placed along the wall between each door. She was surprised to see a likeness of Lawrence on one table among other miniatures of Beaumont's family. She knew Lawrence had his own room here at the manor, but, to have his likeness rendered and displayed showed a modicum of affection for him she had no idea existed. She felt better knowing others were fond of him and that she was not alone in admiring him.

She came upon an opened door where a wall of books beckoned her to enter. The room was the library and spoke of a man's refuge, dark with mahogany shelves, tables, and furniture. There was little color to suggest a lady graced the room, but then Meg determined Lady

Felton probably had her own private library for where she enjoyed her reading.

Drawn to the beautifully bound leather set of volumes, she gently ran her hand over the gilt-lettered titles. Meg loved to read and it excited her to think of the knowledge and adventure waiting to be revealed in each book. There were both classical and contemporary pieces of history, literature, travel, science, poetry, and many of the novels popular among the *bon ton*, including works by Francis Burney, Sir Walter Scott, William Wordsworth, and Lord Byron. It was clear to her a great amount of consideration was put into acquiring the books, and growing the library with new titles.

The volumes of Shakespeare's plays caught Meg's attention and reminded her that she needed to explore his work. She liked how each play was represented in one book. Once, at Hatchard's book store, she saw a large book that contained the complete works of Shakespeare and she remembered thinking what a heavy and burdensome thing it would be to read. Looking at the set of tomes representing the bard's life work, she thought the publisher was a genius to print them up in easy to hold volumes. She could imagine herself carrying one while she traveled or when she sat in the garden. She ran her finger over each book, reading each title, before sentimentally selecting *A Midsummer's Night Dream*.

She sat in the wingback Sheraton chair, easily identified by its cylindrical tapered legs finished in brass caps, and made herself comfortable. Without thinking, she removed her stocking feet from her silk slippers and tucked them under her posterior in her usual way. Her distraction with the small book made her forget she was not in the privacy of her own home, so she thought nothing of sitting so undignified. The tub shaped chair was remarkably comfortable, its wings and back formed a semi-circle and was luxuriously upholstered as one continuous unit. It was easy for Meg to cozy herself into the cushiony seat, especially with a recently stoked fire warming the room. Within minutes, she was flipping through the Shakespearean play, being reminded of her excursion to the Theatre Royal with Lord Atwood. She remembered how gallant his lordship was in shielding her from Lord Spencer's unwanted advances and how very amiable and exciting she found his company. He was all solicitous. Thoughts of him brought goose bumps to her arms and a dreamy look to her eyes. She was so absorbed in her memories she failed to note the man who occupied her mind had entered the library.

Lawrence felt the tension leave his body when he finally found Meg. He had searched for her all morning and was beginning to fear she departed for London, until her cousin assured him she was here, only still abed. Then, he grew concerned over her late rising, especially when he discovered she had retired early from the ball complaining of a head pain. Seeing her with a healthy resolve, passing her time reading, assured him she suffered no ill effects from her aching head. He took a moment to take her measure sitting with her feet pulled under her bottom.

Her elbow was propped on the side arm of her chair, with her head at rest on the pedestal made from her forearm and fist. One of her rich chocolate coils of hair had fallen forward and now rested against her cheek. She was so preoccupied with her reading that she did not notice Lawrence until his feet were planted near her own discarded kid slippers.

Meg became startled when an unexpected pair of Hessian boots came into her view. Frightened, she thrust the leather tome she was reading at her intruder, as though a bug had landed on her lap. She looked up in time to see Lawrence hopping back out of harm's way and blocking the book that came close to hitting him in the nether regions. She crimsoned in embarrassment.

Lawrence saw Meg's blush and bent down to pick up the book that nearly had him blushing. Unfortunately for him, Meg also decided to reach for the book laying at her feet. Their heads collided, striking each other with more force than seemed possible.

Meg grabbed her throbbing forehead and then gasped when she saw she had once again bloodied his lordship's nose. She burst out of her seat, almost tripping on her dress, alarmed at the excessive dark crimson streaming towards his mouth. She stood paralyzed watching him pinch the bridge of his nose while tipping his head back and was drawn to action when she saw him pull forth, with his free hand, the fine piece of linen he kept in his waistcoat pocket. Meg quickly took from her sleeve her own pristine linen and swapped it with his cloth before he knew what she was about, "Please, my lord, take mine. It is not right your linen should be ruined because of my clumsiness."

Lawrence could not argue without creating more of a bloody mess, so he took her sweet-smelling handkerchief and pressed it against his nose. Once he felt the applied pressure ebb the flow of his blood, he lowered his head to excuse himself, but the devastation he saw on Meg's face stopped him. He removed the perfumed cloth from his wound and refolded the square to press a clean portion back to his injury. He was pleased to see the laced handkerchief was not stained, though he was sure blood marked his nose. He was not so vain that tidying himself took precedence over Meg's feelings, so he shoved the soiled linen into his waistcoat and then took Meg's hand in his own. He looked into her eyes, "My dearest Meg, do not repine so, I am not injured in the least, aside from my pride."

Meg could not look at him, for she felt her embarrassment extremely. Her eyes began to pool with unshed tears.

"Will you not look at me, Meg?"

Lawrence's calm voice tugged at Meg's heart and she found she could not refuse him. She looked up to find his eyes sparkling with amusement. His admiration mesmerized her until she felt his palms on her face. She felt him tenderly wipe away the fallen tears on her cheeks with his thumbs. Her eyes widened when she saw him bring his lips to her own. She was so shocked at his indiscretion that the chaste kiss was over before she knew what had happened.

Lawrence quickly released her and stepped back having heard Sir Marcus's and Lord Felton's voice echoing down the hall. He left her without a proper *by-your-leave*, but she heard him greet her father and Lord Felton when he passed them in the hall. All the while, Meg stood transfixed in the spot where he left her in her stocking feet. She stared at the empty threshold and touched her lips with her fingertips, trying to determine if what transpired was a dream.

“Meg!" exclaimed Alicia. "Where have you been? Lord Atwood and I have been searching for you all afternoon.”

“Indeed, for what purpose was I so heartily sought out? I did not know the whereabouts of Felton’s guests was a requirement for one’s stay.”

“Don’t be pompous, Meg. Lord Atwood merely sought you out believing you would enjoy to tour Beaumont's properties with me. He offered his services as guide. When we were unable to locate you, I suggested we defer our ride until tomorrow morning. Now I have confessed my motives, pray tell me, what were yours for avoiding us?”

“I was not avoiding you, Alicia. I simply did not cross paths with you. My afternoon was spent conversing with my parents. I did my best, to no avail I might add, to change their minds regarding our prolonged visit. They are quite determined to stay here for an undisclosed amount of time. They did not relent, even when I reminded them I had engagements with Simon. I am flummoxed as to why they stand firm on this issue, though I admit I am not disappointed to miss finishing the Season. I am weary and long to return to our country home for a respite."

"Then, you should be happy to be here with me for you know that I am prodigiously good company and am usually effectual in pulling you out of your doldrums. Why, may I ask, are you so put out?"

"Who said I am put out?"

"I do. Now tell your loving cousin, what has discommoded you?"

"He kissed me," confessed Meg.

"Who?"

Meg realized they were still in the hallway where anyone might hear them, so she pulled on her cousin's arm until she reached her room's threshold. Then, she opened the door, forcefully pushed her cousin into her sitting room, and closed the door behind her in great haste. Alicia was surprised to see Meg turn the key in the door to secure its lock.

"Well, this must be serious for you to be so agitated. Tell me everything."

"There is not much to tell, Alicia. I was in the library where Lord Atwood startled me. I accidentally dropped the book I was reading and we hit our heads when we both bent down to retrieve the book."

"Is that when he kissed you?"

"No, that is when I bloodied his nose."

"Meg! Tell me you did not!"

"I am afraid I did, Alicia. I tell you I was completely mortified."

"But, you said he kissed you."

"He did. I think he was trying to console me. You see, I was quite distraught being the cause of his injury. I am still upset over the whole ordeal."

"Ordeal? Oh dear, did you not enjoy his kiss, Meg?"

Meg's brows furrowed while she contemplated the question, "I do not know. I do not think it was a proper kiss, for it ended before it ever began."

"Surely, he did not repulse you?"

"No, Alicia. I was not repulsed, but the man does cause me great unrest."

"Well, you must allow yourself another kiss, a proper kiss to assess your true feelings."

"I do not think it wise. I misread his lordship's attentions before and do not wish to do so again. He is only amusing himself with me and I do not wish to engage in those type of games. I am no coquette or wanton, you know."

"But Meg, do you not know that his lordship wishes to pay his addresses to you?"

"Who told you such a ridiculous *taradiddle*?"

"Why, he did."

"What did you say?"

Meg spent the next hour in discourse with her cousin. She went from a state of incredulity to fury. She could not believe her ears. It seemed his lordship had determined he indeed admired her and expected her to accept his addresses. What unmitigated gall. Where was the courtship and professions of love? More important, where was his apology for causing her misery these past weeks? As much as Alicia proclaimed Lord Atwood's sincerity, Meg refused to believe it. Surely her cousin misunderstood what he said. She remembered his many scowls and rebukes; and aside from today's kiss, she could only remember his censure on the few excursions where they kept company, "No, Alicia. He offers nothing more than friendship."

Meg knew Lawrence possessed all the traits of a true gentleman. He was kind, charming, and gallant. He would not intentionally misrepresent himself to her, so she accepted any misunderstanding lay at her door. His failure to proclaim himself at the Davenport Ball was proof enough he had no serious interest in her. Her own experiences persuaded her when the time came, like all gentlemen of the *ton*, Viscount Atwood would pay his addresses to a demure debutante, "No," she told Alicia. "I will not be made the fool again."

"Enough, Meg, I am weary of this argument and wish not to be the interloper. I leave it to you and Lord Atwood to examine and resolve your relationship."

"We have no relationship!"

"Take care, Meg. Lord Atwood is known to be a gentleman and if you rebuff him, he will honor your wishes, regardless of his own. Why if you truly have no feelings for the man, perhaps, I shall venture to discover if he and I could suit. What shall it be?"

Meg was astounded and angry. She wanted to warn her cousin away from him, but her pride kept her from so doing, "If his admiration is so inconstant, then it is better to learn of it now. For if not you, surely another young lady would steal him away."

"I am no thief, Meg. Perchance, you confess your true feelings for the man, if you believe him to belong to you."

"Please stop, Alicia, for I fear I have the headache."

"I am truly sorry, dear cousin, if I am the cause. I shall leave you to rest before we ready for supper."

"I think I am too overwrought. Would you mind extending my regrets and have a tray sent up to me? I plan to retire early after I finish my correspondence. Mama has allowed me to pen Simon a note explaining my absence from Town. I am permitted to invite him to join us here at Beaumont Manor. Mama will include my letter with her own. Lord Felton has promised to expediently dispatch the letter to London in the morning by messenger."

"As you wish, Meg. Will you join me and his lordship tomorrow morning to tour Beaumont's properties?"

Meg hesitated and before she could speak, Alicia interjected, "You harm no one but yourself in hiding yourself away. Eventually, you will have to resolve these emotions you have for Lord Atwood, be it indifference or affection. Why not confront and settle your feelings for the man or are you too afraid?"

Meg's temper got the better of her, "You may tell his lordship I would be pleased to join his company in the morning."

Alicia smiled at how well she managed her cousin. She made her exit before Meg could change her mind. Alicia was determined to see Meg happy even if it meant causing her some minor discomfort.

Astounded to see her mistress awake and sitting at her escritoire, Meg's abigail almost dropped the pitcher of warm water she was carrying. Meg had risen exceptionally early to pen the note to Simon she had forgotten to write the night before because thoughts of Lawrence distracted her. She was nudged awake from a deep slumber with the memory of her failed task and rose quickly to write her note. She was so preoccupied with composing her letter, she did not know Mary entered her room until she heard her gasp, "Why, miss, you are up early!"

Meg sought out her surprised maid the moment she heard her shriek. The sight of Mary struggling to keep the pitcher of water she was carrying from spilling brought a consoling smile to Meg's face.

"I must break my fast, Mary, and have little time to do it for I am riding with Lord Atwood and my cousin this morning. A cup of hot chocolate and a slice of toast will do nicely. I do not wish to be late, so I will attend to my own toilette while you see to my meal."

"Of course, miss." Mary placed the pitcher of warm water and fresh towels she brought for Meg's morning ablutions on the toilette table. Then, she went to open the clothes press to remove her mistress's riding habits before leaving to fetch Meg's morning meal, "Which one, miss, the merino blue or emerald green?"

"The blue, thank you, Mary. Oh, and Mary, make sure my mama receives this note to include in her own letter to Mr. Ware. She is expecting it."

"Very good, miss."

Chapter Thirteen

Descending the main staircase, Meg saw Lawrence pacing near the bottom of the steps. He was looking extremely handsome in his double-breasted coat of superfine dark-blue cloth, buckskin riding breeches, and polished Hessian boots. He stopped mid-stride, having sensed her approach and looked up to find her making her way to him. His attentions made her nervous and she inadvertently came to a halt. She felt as though she was on display like a performer and then almost laughed, recalling how she had seen other debutantes feign a pose when they thought they were under a gentleman's examination. Many ladies under scrutiny would use the opportunity to posture for their admirers, striking a pensive pose by cupping their chin in the v of their thumb and forefinger, while staring off as if they were deep in thought. Meg had no interest in performing, so she simply made her salutation, "Good morning, my lord. I trust I have not kept you and my cousin waiting?"

Lawrence thought Meg looked exquisite in her blue merino riding habit. The military-style suit boasted gold epaulettes with gold-braided piping and frog fastenings decorating the front of her jacket and halfway up her sleeves. Her high collar was trimmed with lace. Around her neck she wore a soft muslin cravat tied in a bow and on her head sat a matching shako hat perched at a perfect angle. Finding his heart thump a tad faster, Lawrence needed to take a calming breath before he answered, "Not at all, Miss Deneham. Your cousin is outside. She informed me she waits in her element among the cattle." Lawrence grinned and Meg laughed at the indecorous but truthful remark, one surely professed by her cousin.

Meg continued to make her way down the stairs, "She is very fond of horses, my lord, and a true equestrian. Her skills are remarked upon by lovers of the hunt. I know of no other female who can equal her aptitude in the saddle."

"Interesting, she says the same of you."

"She is all that is complimentary, my lord, but the truth will be revealed during our jaunt."

"Jaunt, Miss Deneham? Your cousin assures me you and she are more than capable of exercising your mounts. Yesterday, she spoke to one of Beaumont's groomsmen and with his help, marked out a course that might unseat a man. Should I re-plot our trail?"

Lawrence's sincere concern for her safety had her smiling brightly up at him when she reached the landing,

"That is not necessary, my lord. My cousin is very aware of my abilities."

Lawrence couldn't help but return Meg's infectious smile. He proffered his arm to her and was not taken aback when he saw Meg's smile falter. Alicia had confided to him her cousin had serious doubts regarding the sincerity of his affections, so when Meg balked at accepting his escort, he raised an eyebrow as if to say, *"Well, Miss Deneham?"* Much to his relief, he found his haughty behavior effectual in persuading her to place her hand on his arm.

They exited the house and Lawrence walked Meg over to a mounting block. He ordered the nearby ostler to bring forward the chestnut bay mare he personally selected for her from Beaumont's stables and watched to see if she liked the mount he chose for her. The exquisite well-formed animal was at least fifteen hands tall and when he saw Meg's pleasure at having the mare presented to her, he barely maintained his own exuberance at seeing her excitement, "My lord! She is beautiful!"

Her obvious appreciation for the animal pleased him and though he tried to remain impervious to her infectious enthusiasm, he could not keep his lips from twitching and stretching, no doubt, revealing the grin he was trying hard to conceal. Not wanting to mirror her giddy display, he tried to check his laughter by soberly remarking, "Beaumont owns a fine stable, Miss Deneham. I am glad you are happy with my selection. The mare has spirit, but an experienced rider will have no trouble with her."

He watched her move to stand in front of the magnificent animal to pet its nose and coo some sweet words of adoration. Lawrence could not keep from grinning when the mare dipped its head to manipulate Meg into rubbing it. She laughed at the horse's prompting and acquiesced before returning to the mounting block. With her permission, Lawrence assisted her onto her sidesaddle and then walked over to mount his own steed. He turned at the sound of Alicia's mare whinnying and saw her holding the high stepping mare in place, "I hope you are ready for some exercise. Yesterday, I spoke to Beaumont's head groomsman and with his help, I plotted a course I am told will present an amazing view. It is rumored Beaumont's property is unrivaled and I am anxious to see it. I expect to make an adventure for us with a good run and a few jumps. What say you both? Are you up to the challenge?"

Meg smiled at her cousin's enthusiasm and then looked at Lawrence for his agreement, "Canter on fair conqueror. I will follow where you lead."

Lawrence did his best not to cringe. He had hoped Meg would balk at her cousin's plans, but it seemed the ladies were both adept riders. He considered his own skills merely adequate. Since he came into his title, Felton had him engaging and learning all those attributes associated with living the life of a gentleman, areas previously neglected to him as a commoner. In his growing years, he had little opportunity to ride, hunt, fence, or box, since his family lived on the meager earnings gained through teaching. His mother could ill afford lessons, much less own and stable a horse. He did not begin learning how to ride or any of the other pursuits engaged by the titled, until two years ago when he came into his inheritance and Felton took him under his wing. The earl worked judiciously to bring him up to par, hiring instructors and taking him on daily rides that had him jumping logs and streams. He was an enthusiastic and attentive student, and with Felton's encouragement, he took his first fence. The exhilaration he felt when he landed without falling gave him confidence and from that moment on, he found he was at ease in the saddle, at least until today. There was a mischievous nature in Alicia that made him question his abilities to keep up with her. He feared his growing doubts would unman him in front of the lady he was so desperately trying to impress.

Lawrence watched Alicia, with reins in hand, give a gentle slap to her mare as she pushed her heel into her horse's flank to start her into a run. She rode off as though a battle cry was heralded and within seconds, Meg followed suit. Lawrence sat in wonder at their intrepidness, until the melody of their laughter floated back to him. He quickly kicked his own heels and sped off to catch them. Bent over his steed's neck, he raced to close the gap between him and his charges. The small party traversed the east lawns and galloped toward the dense forest of Beaumont. The ground was dry since it had not rained in over a fortnight, so Lawrence was not concerned about injuring Beaumont's cattle. He knew this parcel of lawn to be clear of rabbit and gopher burrows, posing little threat of injury to their horses. Unlike the trodden lanes and other areas where ruts and holes were prominent, there was little chance of their mounts missing a step and breaking a leg. Lawrence was sure Alicia was aware of this fact for she kept her horse unchecked, racing her mare towards the fence bordering the lawns. It was obvious when Alicia spurred her horse she had no intention of using the gate to cross over into the wooded forest, but planned to jump the beech wood fence. The thought panicked Lawrence and he feared for her safety. He watched her lean over her horse's neck as she approached the three foot fence and gasped. His whole body immediately tensed seeing Alicia's mare take flight. He hadn't realized he was holding his breath until Alicia landed safely and he exhaled. Then, his breath hitched again when Meg followed her cousin over the planked barrier. He sat in wonder over their proficiency, until he was overcome with embarrassment at seeing the ladies on the other side of the fence, waiting for him to make his own jump.

Whether from the amazing sight of the ladies' jumps or outright fear for their safety, Lawrence had unconsciously jerked on his reins slowing his horse to a canter. The thought of showing himself poorly discomfited him and sparked him into action. He quickly loosened his grip on the leather straps and gave his horse a much-needed heel to get him to leap. He nearly unseated himself when instead of focusing on the ground before him, he shifted his body to search out Meg. He knew he was in danger when her eyes alighted with concern. His quick reflexes kept him from falling and with less grace than he wished, he came to a stop. He patted his steed's neck, whispering his sincerest thanks.

"O, ho! My Lord Atwood! You quite put the fear in me." Though chuckling, Lawrence could hear the distress in Alicia's voice. She gently chided him, "You should have told me if you preferred not to jump. I would never have put such a burden upon you."

"Do not stress yourself, Miss Deneham. It was my wonder of the two of you that almost tossed me from my saddle. I am quite capable of keeping up, as long as I keep my wits about me."

"Very good, my lord, but we will take it easy through the woods, since I am not familiar with them and wish to give our mounts a rest." Alicia waved her arm in an arc to bring attention to their colorful scenery, "The silver birch trees and vibrant bluebells carpeting the ground with color are beautiful. I am glad we ventured here. Perhaps, you prefer to lead, my lord, since you no doubt have ventured here before?"

"For that reason alone, I relinquish the role to you, Miss Deneham. I would prefer to see the woods fresh through your eyes. Besides, I find I have the better view, taking up the rear behind the both of you."

Alicia laughed at his bold and teasing remark while Meg blushed, fanning her eyelashes down in embarrassment. Meg knew Lord Atwood's remark was a mere flirtation, but it made her diffident, especially when she realized how much she wanted his attentions to be genuine. She wondered if she would ever find his company companionable again, without her conscious warning her not to open her heart to hurt.

Lawrence noted Meg's cheeks color and chided himself for his witticism. He knew Meg questioned his sincerity and would see such teasing remarks as disingenuous. He needed to be more careful and not use flirtations to win her favor.

They walked their horses under the canopy constructed from the tall trees and their thickly leafed branches towering over them. The temperature was cool for like an umbrella, the covering blocked out the sun's penetrating warmth. Below them lay a lush cover of wild bluebells laying vibrant against their evergreen foliage. They quietly rode in tandem making their way through the dense green forest of gnarled oak and silver birch trees whose white trunks rose high over their heads like Greek pillars. Sunlight filtered through the tree branches, illuminating their trail and the dust particles that floated around them. A profound feeling of peace and tranquility overcame them and the spiritual feeling invoked them into silence. Lawrence was sure they were all of the same mind, where to speak would break the magic of the moment.

They were momentarily blinded by the bright sun when they left the protection of the woods to enter the rich and grassy vale where hedgerows divided the property into blocks. Bushes and oak trees dotted the landscape, and the sounds of sheep baying and cattle mooing resonated from where the animals were seen grazing in the distance. Before Lawrence could ask, "Where to?" Alicia spurred her horse into a gallop. Lawrence did not wait for Meg to follow her cousin. He started his own horse into a canter and then into an all out gallop. He was determined to be the one to finish first to await the others to join him. He knew he had the faster and larger of the mounts, so he raced with abandon. He gave his steed his legs and sped past Alicia to take the first hedge. He did not stop until he took the stream weaving through the valley, smiling with glee when Alicia and Meg joined him on the other side. He chuckled when he saw their delight at his proficiency and was glad they took no offense to his outrageous victory.

"Very well done, my lord," exclaimed Alicia. "I see your male pride could not be governed."

"So it seems. But confess, Miss Deneham. You would much prefer a gentleman with pride than one without."

Alicia asked, "You have become philosophical, my lord?"

"No, not at all, but I have become hungry. Come, it is time to let our mounts and ourselves rest. Cook prepared us a repast. Let us take the hill and enjoy it. I am sure the view will be rewarding."

"Very good, my lord," replied Alicia. "And I will give you your due in saying yes, I would prefer a man with pride than one without."

Lawrence was glad the place they chose to respite was free of rocks. He helped the ladies dismount and then untied the rolled blanket that was secured behind his saddle. He laid it on the thick grass for the ladies to sit and set out the parcels Cook packed. While they arranged their food, he led the horses over to an ancient oak tree whose leafy branches offered them protection from the sun's heat and dropped their reins onto the ground to keep them from wandering off. He left them to munch on the thick grass while he saw to his own hunger.

"You are quiet, Meg," remarked Alicia. "Are you not enjoying yourself?"

Meg opened her mouth to respond, then realized she did not know how to answer. The truth was she could think of no other place she would rather be than in Lord Atwood's company, but her fear of being hurt kept her from enjoying herself. Alicia saw her balk at answering and knew her cousin was troubled. She patted Meg's hand and offered her opinion, "Give him a chance, Meg. I do not think he misrepresents himself. I do not believe he ever did. I suppose he did not initially understand his feelings and rather than confess his ineptitude, he did what all men do when they are first assaulted with an emotion grander than anything they have ever experienced. They draw back and many times run away. The brave ones, the smart ones know the risk is worthwhile and always return in earnest to press their suit."

Alicia heard Lawrence approach and refrained from further conversation. She retrieved her hand from Meg's and offered her a supporting smile. They both looked up when he reached them.

Lawrence feared he intruded upon a *tête-à-tête* and felt quite awkward. He knew if he retreated, it would make the situation even more uncomfortable, so he asked, "What delights did Cook prepare for us? I admit I am more than ready to assuage my hunger."

He was happy when Meg offered the reply for it had not gone unnoticed by him that she had held her tongue throughout their excursion. Only an occasional and reluctant giggle and smile proved she was enjoying herself. Lawrence was beginning to fear his cause was lost until Meg finally broke her silence to reply to his question, "We have cucumber and ham sandwiches, my lord, Cotswold cheese, biscuits, sliced apple pieces, and what looks like a peach tart. Will that satisfy you?"

"For food, yes." Meg blushed at his teasing banter. Before the situation became unbearable, he announced, "And we have a colambre of wine of which I saw to myself.

I can assure you the burgundy is one of Felton's finest. Shall we eat?"

Meg and Alicia heartily agreed. Lawrence joined them on the blanket to commence their picnic and soon they fell into a camaraderie, eating and drinking while they bantered. They spoke of the majestic countryside, the society known to them all, and to Alicia's delight, her father's breeding farm. It pleased Lawrence to see Meg finally relaxed in his company and he hated to end their excursion. He was about to suggest they collect their belongings when Alicia announced, "You must excuse me while I look for some privacy."

It was not uncommon to make a discreet and rustic call to nature when traveling, so Lawrence said, "Of course, Miss Deneham. I ask you not to venture too far as these hills may or may not be home to highwaymen or hermits. Call if you need my protection."

Alicia had no need to relieve herself, but thought to give her cousin and suitor an opportunity to be alone. She made her way further up the hill and disappeared into the trees flanking it.

Lawrence noted the glint in Alicia's eyes when she proclaimed her need for privacy. He was sure she was offering him a moment alone with Meg and was not about to waste the opportunity to press his suit. As soon as Alicia cleared his view, he turned to Meg, only to find her beginning to rise. He quickly stood and helped her to her feet. He watched her smooth her skirt and then he closed the space between them and took her hand. He led her towards the panoramic scene of the vale.

She remarked, "It is a beautiful view, is it not?"

"Yes, it is."

Meg felt his eyes on her and turned to him, "I wish you would not play fast and free with me, my lord. I am not experienced or an engaging flirt. I fear I am too dull to master the art of it."

"You are far from dull, Meg. I have always enjoyed your company." Lawrence took both of Meg's hands in his own. She watched as though she was an observer rather than a participant and felt his thumbs massage the back of her hands. Her eyes were locked on his own. She watched him take a deep breath and waited for him to speak, "I know I hurt you, Meg, and for that I am extremely sorry. I did not play you false. I only took longer than you to understand my feelings. You stirred my emotions and agitated me beyond belief from the first time I saw you. Only recently have I come to understand this overwhelming feeling I have for you is love. I hope you will allow me the opportunity to prove my sincerity. Will you let me court you, Meg?"

Speechless, Meg could do nothing other than look at Lawrence whose eyes were locked on her own. She thought he spoke genuinely and whether she ought to or not, she believed him. She could see he awaited her answer, but her mouth was too dry to voice a response, so she smiled.

Lawrence waited breathlessly for her answer. He expected words, but the effervescent smile she produced was more than enough to satisfy him. He enthusiastically embraced her, wrapping her up in his arms, waiting to see if his advances were truly desired. He was extraordinarily relieved when Meg, with her smile stretching even wider, wrapped her own arms around his neck. He kissed her and when she pressed her lips more firmly against his own, he embraced her tighter and deepened his kiss.

"Are we ready to depart, Cousin, or am I to take myself away again?"

Alicia's voice broke their embrace. Meg blushed at her cousin's coarse interruption, while Lawrence answered her question, "We are quite ready, Miss Deneham. By the way, I heartily thank you for allowing us the time we needed to resolve our issues."

Alicia laughed, "Ah, so that was what you were doing."

Meg went and grabbed her laughing cousin and pulled her towards the picnic area, telling Lawrence over her shoulder that they would pack up their goods while he saw to the horses. Lawrence grinned watching Meg reprimand her cousin for her less than tactful inquiry and then went to collect their mounts.

They meandered back over hill, through vale and forest, until they entered the gravel lane to Beaumont's manor home. The return trip was full of light banter and Lawrence felt that his cup runneth over. Surely, the road to Meg's heart would be a smooth one now she knew his intentions were honorable. He wondered how long before he could pay his addresses to her. He was so distracted with his thoughts he did not understand Meg's shout until she rode off. He watched her gallop away towards a newly arrived visitor dismounting his horse at Beaumont's front steps. Meg's bellow identified the man as her ardent suitor, the ever-relentless Simon Ware. Lawrence looked at Alicia, who keeping pace by his side, simply shrugged her shoulders. He returned his gaze to the happy reunion and unconsciously pulled on his reins, startling his horse to stop. Alicia checked her own horse to stay next to him, "Come now, my lord. Surely you knew Meg invited Simon to join us. Do not be ill at ease. You know that they are lifelong friends."

"If," thought Lawrence, *"Alicia is trying to ease my concerns, she has failed miserably."* He loosened his grip on his reins, heeled his steed and made his way to join the happy couple.

Chapter Fourteen

Lawrence pulled on his reins to bring his horse to an abrupt stop before the manor. Uncomfortably, he watched while Meg's lifelong friend grasped her by the waist to remove her from her sidesaddle and then embrace her with an enthusiastic hug. The scene had him jerking his leather straps. His heated emotions spooked his horse, causing the beast to snort and sidestep. Alicia, who kept by his side, called out a warning for him to mind his temper before his horse bucked him off his fine seat. Blushing from Alicia's rant, he quickly dismounted and went to assist her down from her mare, happily relinquishing his and her reins to the attending ostlers, before joining Meg and her ardent suitor.

The Earl and Countess of Felton, having been apprised by their stalwart butler of a newly arrived guest, exited the manor to welcome him. Lawrence fumed watching Meg offer Simon another cheerful greeting before introducing him to her hosts. He thought the display overmuch for a supposed friendship and worked to calm his rising temper while Simon was made welcome by his hosts. He begrudgingly observed the proceedings, then trailed behind the party as Felton commanded them into the manor to join his other guests in the parlour.

Apparently, Mr. Simon Ware was second in line to an earldom and while his elder brother would most likely ascend to the title, Simon's own livelihood was secure in his grandmother's bequest to him. He was to take ownership of an affluent piece of property in the county of Cheshire on his thirtieth birthday. The only caveat to his inheritance was he must be married. Lawrence surmised his ardent pursuit of Meg this Season was attributed to his need to comply with his grandmother's wishes, but anyone with eyes could see Simon's affection for Meg was genuine. He remembered Simon's anger at seeing Meg's distress at the Davenport Ball and looking back, he was lucky Simon did not call him out for importuning her. After all, at the time, Lawrence was *persona non-grata* with Sir Marcus and Simon could have demanded satisfaction from him for bothering Meg. As if one imbroglio this Season with Spencer was not enough, Lawrence could easily have had two scandals attributed to him. Incredulous.

Lawrence's intrusive snort turned everyone's heads to him for the source. He gasped at their affronted looks and his face crimsoned from embarrassment. An emotion that quickly turned to anger when he saw Meg's longtime suitor grin at his discomfort. Meg's wide-eyed amazement did little to diminish his temper. No doubt she was surprised that, unlike the others, he was not charmed by the gallantry of her steadfast admirer. It took every ounce of his fortitude to display an air of indifference when nothing was farther from the truth. He had grown tired watching the woman he loved beam with adoration for a man he considered his adversary. It was obvious to him how much Meg wanted everyone to like Simon and he was sure she would have taken it as a personal insult if anyone took Simon in dislike. His accidental snort burst forth when Meg failed to laugh at Simon's glib remark. Her obvious confusion and frown was enough to generate the derisive noise, though he regretted his outburst the moment it drew everyone's attention. He owed Lady Felton a debt of gratitude for redirecting the attention from him back to Simon by expressing her regrets that Simon missed the festival ball. A discourse erupted among the party, as the countess intended, on all that transpired during the fete, until she put an end to it by suggesting they all retire to rest before dinner. Lawrence was glad for the respite, for oddly, watching Meg interact with Simon had wearied him.

How long had he been woolgathering? Hadn't he just sat down to eat? Lawrence didn't remember any of the dinner courses served before him or if he had eaten anything. He began to poke at the neglected plate of dessert confection in front of him and speculated he must have made only a monosyllabic contribution to the table conversation. Watching Simon and Meg grin and chuckle at each other had exasperated and kept him from eating. Their friendly banter and camaraderie irked him. It seemed whatever Simon said was amusing and he began to wonder if Meg found his conversation equally exceptional. *Exactly how often did Meg smile in his company compared to Simon's?* He was about to tally an impossible count when he saw Lady Felton rise from the table, the signal for the other ladies to follow her into the parlour for their after-dinner tea, leaving the gentlemen to drink their port in private. Lawrence was glad to see the ladies depart, if for no other reason than to see Simon separated from Meg.

Lord Felton directed his footman to fill each man's glass and raised his glass as he said, "I suggest we drink our port with due haste, gentlemen, since I intend to join my wife as soon as possible."

Sir Marcus laughed, "You would think that you were still a newlywed, Felton."

"You are not one to talk Sir Marcus. Your attendance upon Lady Deneham is well remarked upon by the *ton*."

Sir Marcus blushed and immediately turned to Lawrence to deflect the attention away from himself, "My niece and daughter spoke of your ride today, Atwood.

Felton gave me a tour of the home farm and his tenant property, but we did not venture to the east. I will have to explore that territory before I leave."

"I will be happy to guide you, Sir Marcus," offered Edward. "Will tomorrow do?"

"Yes, thank you, Felton, but mind you, I will prefer the gates to the fences."

Simon laughed, "Who is to blame for taking the fences? Alicia or Meg?"

Sir Marcus raised an eyebrow to Lawrence in inquiry. The gesture broke his resolve of holding Simon in contempt, especially after witnessing the man's friendly manner and clear affection for the Deneham family. Chuckling, Lawrence confessed Miss Alicia Deneham was the culprit and leader in their riding excursion. He described their race across the east lawns and vale, recalling their arduous jumps over fences, hedgerows, and streams. The conversation prompted Sir Marcus and Simon to recount many of the girls' equestrian escapades and by the time the gentlemen rose to join the ladies in the parlour, Lawrence found it difficult not to like Simon Ware. He was a pleasant and unpretentious man. It was easy to see why Meg enjoyed his company. He silently groaned knowing when they rejoined the ladies he would, once again, have to endure watching the woman he admired look adoringly at another man. He expected the evening to be intolerable.

Lawrence was about to make his way to the breakfast parlour when one of the earl's footmen intercepted him to present him with the silver salver on which a folded note lay. Lawrence picked up the unsealed paper and quickly read its contents. He was surprised to read the earl requested an interview with him. It was uncommon to be summoned to his private suite instead of his study, so before worry could set in, he hastily made his way to him. He did not know what to expect when he entered his lordship's room, but it was not to find the earl under the ministrations of his valet, Jenkins. The scene pacified him, knowing Felton would not be standing still to be dressed if he had urgent news to impart. He took himself to the window while the earl finished dressing. The window was the best place to view the immaculate knot garden that took its design from the tapestry residing in the Green State Room. Beaumont's mother had chosen the design and supervised the creation of the garden that over the years provided a peaceful retreat for the manor's owners and their guests. Low standing boxwood hedges created geometric shapes and each shape was filled with flowers and herbs. Only from a bird's eye view could one marvel at the color and exquisiteness of the symmetrical design.

From his vantage point, Lawrence spied the marquis strolling through the garden and felt a pang of guilt, "I see Beaumont is up early as usual. I expect the book tucked under his arm is Wordsworth. I am sorry I have not inquired of him. He has been absent from our party. He has not been ill, has he?"

Edward turned to him, "No, Atwood. Just weary. The festival tired him out, so now he chooses his solitude to our party. His wit is as sharp as ever, though I have to acknowledge he is slowing down."

"He must be very pleased you will be presenting him with an heir to continue his line."

"Indeed," Edward grinned knowing his uncle was more than pleased. He was ecstatic about the arrival of his child. He walked over to stand next to Lawrence and looked out the window to search for his uncle. He watched, along with Lawrence, as the marquis disappeared through the secret portal that led to his private garden. Only the heirs to the Beaumont title and their wives were privy to its location, though an exception was made for Lawrence for whom the marquis held a strong affection.

"I am working on my own secret garden at my home, Felton. I do not have the ivy, shrubbery, or trees to hide its location as yet, but the masons are working on its enclosure while we speak."

"A Garden of Eden will serve you and your future wife well, Atwood. Anne and I have benefited from the peace and solitude it offers."

Lawrence wondered why Edward had summoned him, "Did you need something of me, Felton?"

"No, not at all. I only wished to apologize for not redirecting Ware's request last night for an archery tournament. I know I have not had the opportunity to introduce you to the sport and regret you will not be shown to advantage."

Lawrence remembered how the tournament came to fruition after rejoining the ladies in the parlour. They had entered the room in time to hear Lady Deneham exclaim how there were a number of pursuits where ladies could outshine any man. It seemed the ladies were in earnest conversation besmirching the performances of many gentlemen of their acquaintance. The tournament was scheduled when Simon insisted their opinion be tested with a contest between the sexes. The endearing look Simon gave Meg, recalled Lawrence to his present conversation, "You know about Ware's admiration for Miss Margaret Deneham?"

"It has been of long-standing to my knowledge."

"Indeed," after a moment, Lawrence added, "but unrequited."

"I should hope," chuckled Edward, "since she is the one you wish to marry."

"Do not concern yourself about the tournament, Felton. I am quite content watching the competition from the sidelines. I am sure I can find other ways to impress Miss Deneham. I do not fear Ware's suit, I only envy his companionship with her. He has had an unfair advantage in having known her for far more years than I."

"Which might be why you have her heart and not her camaraderie, Atwood. I believe she treats him more like a relative than an admirer."

"We aristocrats are known to marry our cousins, Felton. You have not eased my mind with your observation."

Edward laughed, "I would not concern yourself yet, Atwood. I believe in the end, love will prevail."

Chapter Fifteen

Meg was finishing her cup of hot chocolate when Alicia pranced into her private suite. She was impeccably dressed in a bottle green riding habit and Meg sighed over her own dishabille, "Cousin, must you make me feel inadequate? How can you be so cheerful and up to meet the world at this early hour?"

Alicia responded to Meg's complaints with a burst of chuckles before reminding her, "Did you forget I am taking Simon out to see the properties? You are welcome to come."

"No, thank you. I will be quite content spending some time in the library until you return. It was nice of you to give him a tour, Alicia."

"Nonsense. You know I love to ride, besides, I thought you might like a moment with Lord Atwood. Simon was quite cruel in monopolizing your time yesterday."

"He did no such thing, Alicia."

"Meg, have you told Simon of your feelings for his lordship?"

"He has known since the Davenport Ball. He does not think him worthy of me. He offered for me again."

"Wretched man. How did you answer?"

"I refused of course."

"He took it well I presume?"

"He always does, Alicia, but he refuses to abandon his suit, until he is sure Lord Atwood is worthy of me. I told him I feared Lawrence would misconstrue our relationship and then he chided me for making it easy for the man to win my hand. He insists if Viscount Atwood loves me, then his attentions should not dissuade Lawrence from making an offer for me. I am afraid Simon may have the right of it, Alicia, and perhaps Lawrence's suit is a fickle one."

"You are thinking too much, Meg. Follow your heart, it will not mislead you." Alicia gave her cousin a warm hug and then bid her farewell, "Well, I must be off. Enjoy your time with your viscount."

Lawrence found Meg perusing a familiar book known to him. It was Beaumont's favorite read, a collection of William Wordsworth poems. The marquis had a habit of leaving the volume, usually open on the last page he was reading, on a side table in the library. He always returned later in the afternoon to pick it up to start reading where he had left off. Lawrence expected

Beaumont could quote the poems by heart since he had been reading the same volume from before Lawrence had known him. The presence of the book told him Beaumont was not in his secret garden for he would not have ventured there without his poetry. He smiled, feeling Providence was with him by having the garden empty for him to share it with Meg, "Here you are, Meg. I feared you changed your mind and rode out with your cousin and Mr. Ware after all."

"No. I am not as diligent as Alicia in taking a daily ride. I confess it is in this way I am like your typical timid debutant."

Lawrence laughed, "You cannot fool me, Meg. You are far from timid. I see you have Beaumont's favorite poet in your hands. Are you familiar with Wordsworth?"

"Not enough to quote him, my lord, but I find his prose compelling. He must be a naturalist to be able to capture the beauty and mood of our surroundings."

Smiling, he proffered his hands to help Meg rise and commanded, "Come, I have a secret to show you, but first I must ask whether you can hold quiet on the treasure I am about to show you."

"My lord, is it stolen?"

"No, Meg," he grinned, "I want to show you Beaumont's secret garden. I know it is empty because you are holding the book he takes as companion when he visits and Felton will not accompany his countess there until later in the afternoon."

"I have always wondered where they disappeared to at that time of day, but if it is a secret, how do you come to know of it?"

"Because unlike you, I have an impish nature. When I first arrived here to stay with Beaumont, I became curious to learn where the marquis disappeared in the early morning hours, so I followed him. I thought I was quite stealthy with my spying, but I believe Beaumont knew I followed him because the key to open the concealed door to his secret garden was protruding from its hiding place when I returned to investigate. Felton agrees with my deduction and asked me not to embarrass Beaumont by telling him. He said the marquis would feel guilty for revealing the garden's location to someone other than his heir. Felton explained it was tradition for the garden's location to be revealed to only the Marquis of Beaumont's future heirs and their head gardeners. Obviously Beaumont told Felton who shares the garden with his countess. The earl encouraged me to visit the garden when it is empty as he knew that would be his uncle's wish. I feel very honored Beaumont shares his special retreat with me and trusts me not to reveal its location. Come, I want to share it with you."

"I cannot! I would be trespassing! And you just said Beaumont trusts you not to reveal its location."

"He knows what you mean to me and it would please him to know I shared it with you. Plus, I know I can trust you not to reveal its location to anyone else."

Meg hesitated, but when Lawrence tugged on her arm, her scruples gave way to her curiosity. She relented and did not fight being pulled. Before long, he guided her arm through his and drew her close to him. It seemed as though they were an old married couple taking a stroll and Meg was comforted by the thought.

Lawrence escorted her through the parlour doors opening unto the knot garden. He led her along the gravel path to a point where the lane veered away from the knot garden towards Beaumont's grove of fruit trees. A wall of ivy separated the garden from the orchard. Meg watched in wonder while Lawrence slipped into what seemed to be a solid wall of ivy. Meg realized the secret garden's entrance was hidden because of the illusion of one solid wall. In reality, there were two ivy covered walls running parallel to one another with a portal in the front wall, unrecognizable unless a trespasser was upon it. The parallel walls created a corridor into which Lawrence turned. Meg followed him into the tight passage until they reached a dead end. Then, she watched Lawrence stick his hand into a ivy covered crevice to pull out a tarnished brass key. Lawrence pushed back the overgrown climbing ivy to reveal the door's lock. He inserted the ancient key and within seconds, she was being pushed forward into what seemed like a magical world. All the flowers were in full bloom. Her senses were immediately overwhelmed with vibrant colors and sweet fragrances. Canary daffodils, sprawling powder-blue forget-me-nots, vibrant purple violets, clusters of white crocus, pale yellow primroses, and more varieties filled the floral landscape. She would never have guessed looking from the knot garden, an ivy wall concealed a private and thriving place. Even from the top floors of the manor, this Garden of Eden was shielded from prying eyes by the cover of lush-leafed trees lining its walls. Any spy would think the trees were part of the grove flanking the garden's back wall.

The air was warm and sweet-scented. Butterflies and hummingbirds fluttered around Meg and she laughed when a Peacock butterfly landed on her shoulder, spreading its hind wings to reveal the large decorative eyes it uses to threaten predators. She twirled in delight, extending her arms like a pinwheel, tilting her head back to observe the garden in a kaleidoscope of colors as she spun. She remembered how as a girl she had run amok among the wildflowers at her uncle's country estate to chase butterflies and the memory enhanced her experience.

Lawrence watched the woman he loved delight in nature's beauty. Her laughter was so infectious that he began to chuckle with her. Eager to add to her jejune enjoyment, he grabbed her hand and pulled her over to an old oak tree. A swing fell from its gnarled stout branch. Meg gave no argument when he placed her on the wooden plank and then she reveled in being pulled back on her seat, so gravity would sway her like a pendulum. Each time Lawrence pushed her, she thrust her legs out to propel herself higher into her arc.

Meg thought she was in a fairyland. From her perch, the garden's spectrum of colors danced in her eyes. She was so absorbed with the moment she did not notice she was slowing down until Lawrence stood in front of her. She reluctantly dragged her kid slippers on the ground to stop, not wanting to run into him and watched dumbstruck while he dropped down on one knee in front of her, "I am building my own secret garden at my home in Yorkshire and hope one day my viscountess and I will enjoy the same peace this garden has given Beaumont. It is my greatest desire that you be the woman to enjoy it with me. Tell me, Meg, may I ask your father permission to pay my addresses to you?"

Meg balked. She did not expect his proposal and did not know what to say. She simply stared at him in disbelief. Lawrence watched Meg's astonishment and was surprised at how her reluctance did not offend him, though her silence did make him wary. Calmly, he prompted her with care, "You have no answer for me, Meg?"

"Oh, dear. I am sorry, my lord, but you take me by surprise. It seems too soon, do you not think, to present such an offer?"

"Not to me," retorted Lawrence, his temper rising from thinking Meg's feelings did not equate to his own. "I know my heart, Meg. Perhaps, you do not, or perhaps, your affections lay elsewhere. I understand Ware has offered for your hand."

"Simon is all that is good and honorable, but he knows my affections belong to another."

"Am I the one you love?"

"You have turned my professed affection into love, my lord. It is rather arrogant of you."

Frustrated, Lawrence fervently explained, "What you hear is a reflection of my own feelings, Meg. Do not banter with me. Will you or will you not be my wife?"

"You move too quickly, my lord."

"I do not think so."

"I do not know what to say to you, my lord. Except that I am not ready to commit to a man who finds me unworthy of a courtship. I bid you good day." Upset, Meg rose from her seat and brusquely walked away.

They did not meet again until the archery tournament. Lawrence's temper had diminished little, though his anger was now directed at himself for blindsiding Meg with his proposal. He had come to realize that Meg was right to want a courtship and he regretted that he had not wooed her as he should, though her refusal made him question if he had yet to win her heart. *Did not their kiss seal an understanding between them?* He fretted he had misunderstood.

The more he worried, the more he hated standing idly by while Simon impressed Meg with his archery skills. When it came to sports, he would much rather be a participant than an observer, but he knew a tournament was no place to be introduced to a new skill. It did not take him long to quietly protest Meg's personal instruction from Simon. Surely, he thought the man needn't touch her as often as he did while they took practice shots.

Alicia insisted the two teams be divided by gender. Alicia, Meg, and Lady Deneham made up one team, while Simon, Sir Marcus, and Lord Felton made up the second one. Lawrence stood next to Lady Felton who reclined on a chaise sofa at a safe distance to observe the contest. Two targets were set up at twenty-five yards away. Lord Felton had two of his servants nearby to measure with a string the distance from the arrow to the bull's-eye center should a winner be in question. The women were taking their practice shots. Meg had just taken hers when Lawrence heard Simon remark again to her, "Do not drop your arm after your release, Meg, it is making your arrow drop on the target."

"Simon, if you scold me one more time, I will put this arrow to better use and poke you with it."

Lawrence laughed louder than he intended and drew Simon to turn to him, "Perhaps you would like to join us, Atwood?"

"It would be unfair of me to participate, since I have never tried the sport before, Ware."

"Nonsense," said Lady Deneham. "We are here only to amuse ourselves. You may join the ladies, my lord, since we are the better team. The men require a handicap if they have any chance of winning and your lack of proficiency will even the odds."

Sir Marcus joked, "I do believe, Gentlemen, a challenge has been issued. Do we accept?"

Lord Felton and Simon grinned, nodding their agreement to a wager. Sir Marcus turned to his wife, "We accept, my dear. What are the stakes?"

The ladies conferred, "If we win, then you shall comply with our request for this evening's entertainment. If you win, then your wishes take precedence."

"Sounds fair," replied Sir Marcus. "We men will each take four shots to your three shots apiece. We will give you fifteen minutes to tutor Atwood and then we will begin. Agreed?"

"Agreed," chimed the women in unison.

The fifteen minutes passed quickly and Lawrence felt ill-prepared. He could feel Simon's eyes on him throughout his practice and he was sure he heard the man chuckle now and again. He could not complain of his tutors. All three ladies shared their expertise and while Lawrence had no experience with the sport, he understood the concept well enough. He was ready to deliver his best shot.

It was determined he would shoot last in the order, so he could observe the other player's skills. Meg was first up and her first arrow fell low on the straw-filled target. Simon quickly reminded her not to drop her arm before the arrow met its mark. Lawrence thought Simon's advice accurate based on what he saw, though he wished Simon used a softer tone with Meg. He did not like the man speaking to her as though he had authority over her.

Simon shot first for the gentlemen and settled himself in front of the target. Lawrence watched him take his time to plant his feet so his body was centered over the shooting line. He noted how Simon kept the elbow of his drawing arm high, holding his bow and arrow steady until he was ready to shoot. Simon's singular focus was on the target. When he was ready, he released his fingers on his bowstring to let his arrow fly. He took great satisfaction when his arrow hit the bull's-eye scoring the first point for his team.

Alicia was up next and displayed an innate athleticism. She was far from a hoyden, exhibiting as much grace in sports as a debutante does on the dance floor. She studied her target with a confidence built from years of practice. Her arrow flew straight and found its mark near the perimeter of the bull's-eye. Edward was her opponent in this round. Everyone knew he was a master archer and expected him to take the point. In one fluid move, he pulled taut his bowstring, but his concentration was distracted when he heard his wife cry out in pain. The shriek caused him to prematurely release his arrow. He dropped his bow and frantically ran to his very pregnant wife's side. His team members watched his errant arrow fly wide of the target while the earl fell to his knees before his countess, "Anne, Anne, what ails you?"

Anne held her head down and Edward feared the worst possible scenario. He placed his fingers under her chin to lift her head when she refused to answer him. His anger rose when he saw that she was perfectly fine, "You wretched woman. You are *beyond the pale* putting such a fear in me. What mischief do you delight in?"

Contrite, but determined, Anne whispered, "Oh, Edward, you must help the ladies. I am told if we win, they will ask Mr. Ware to play the pianoforte. They say he has a rare talent, though he never performs publicly. I would so love to hear him."

"Perhaps, I prefer your singing to any of his sonatas."

"But you can command me at will, my lord, while you have no power over him. Please, Edward, it is my wish."

"You underestimate my powers, madam, but I will do your bidding, only because it pleases me to see you happy."

"Thank you, Edward. You are all that is good."

Lady Deneham took the initiative to inquire after her conspirator in crime. She could see the others in the party were growing quite concerned, so she called out, "Is she all right, Felton?"

"Yes. Only a twinge. Nothing of import to worry." He rose to return to the competition, remarking to Alicia, "The point is yours, Miss Deneham. Wc do not redraw simply because one cannot hold their concentration."

Alicia laughed at her easy victory and teased, "I must remember to stay focused, my lord."

Lady Deneham and Sir Marcus competed against one another and both hit the target's bull's-eye. They went into the second round tied. Lawrence was up next and found himself matched with Simon. He took his time, but he had little confidence he would perform well. He mentally reviewed all the steps he needed to follow to ensure any degree of success and was disappointed when his arrow escaped his grasp before he was ready to release it, flying wide of his target. He was grateful no one remarked upon his ill attempt. Simon took his turn and won the point for his team.

Next, came the match between Meg and Lord Felton. While they took their shots, Simon approached Lawrence and discreetly offered, "Make sure your bow and string are vertical to the target. Any deviation will make your shot wide." Lawrence whispered his gratitude to him and then watched him walk away to consult Meg. Lawrence could not help but admit if Simon was not fixated on marrying Meg, then the two of them would get along admirably.

Somehow the teams were tied in the last round, though it looked like a sure victory for the gentleman since Sir Marcus was matched against the novice. Lawrence felt the pressure of having to compete for the win. He took his stance and again, carefully thought about each step he needed to perform. He knocked his arrow on his bowstring, placing his index finger above his arrow, and his middle and third finger below it, curling his three fingers at their first joint around the bowstring. He raised his bow, pushing out his bow arm and then he carefully pulled back on his bowstring feeling his back muscles tense. His nerves got the better of him, making him wonder if he had forgotten something, compelling him to start over, so he released the tension on his bowstring and lowered his bow to compose himself. He took a calming breath before beginning again with a proper stance. Facing the target, he planted one foot on each side of the shooting line in an open position. This time when he pulled back on his bowstring, he remembered to check the vertical alignment of his bow and string as Simon suggested. Then he took aim and when he was ready, released his fingers. The bow's strum reminded him, as Simon was always instructing Meg to do, to hold his position until his arrow hit its mark. It was the closest he had gotten to the target's center and he was immensely satisfied. Lawrence stepped back to watch Sir Marcus prepare to take his final shot for his team.

While Sir Marcus settled himself into position, Lady Deneham remarked, “Marcus dear, do be careful. I would hate to see you suffer for shooting unwisely.”

Simon exclaimed, “Not fair, Lady Deneham, coercion is bad sportsmanship.”

“You speak in riddles, Simon. I only caution my husband because I would hate to see him wretched.”

Sir Marcus seemed oblivious to his wife's warning for his focus never left his target. Everyone watched in anticipation for him to shoot his arrow. Right when he released his fingers to let his arrow fly, a series of harsh coughs broke the silence and his concentration, causing him to jerk his bow. His arrow flew wide of the target's center. It was unnecessary to take a measurement to determine who won the round. The ladies heralded their victory while Simon frowned.

Simon approached his teammates, "Badly done, Gentlemen. It was quite obvious I had treachery on my team. You, my lord, surrendered every win and interfered with at least one of Sir Marcus's shots. If I wasn't so pleased to see Meg happy, I might demand satisfaction."

"I'm with you, Simon," added Sir Marcus, "I was bloody mad with that coughing spell Felton erupted to distract me. I was lucky I did not hit one of his servants. What the deuce was that all about?"

"Come now," explained Simon, "Felton was simply doing his lady wife's bidding. If not for my stellar performance, we would be the *on dit* of the Season. Surely, you know the ladies will be boasting of their victory, once they return to Town."

He laughed when he saw Felton's and Sir Marcus's bemused faces turn sour, "Well, I hope you are ready to comply with their wishes for tonight's entertainment."

Edward smirked. He knew it was Simon who would pay their price for the day's loss, "Come, let us take our refreshments."

Chapter Sixteen

Anne's body began to tremble again, so she stiffened her spine and focused on calming herself to keep from spilling the cup of tea she held in her hand. Three times she tried to bring her delicate Sevres cup to her mouth and three times Lady Deneham's quips had her laughing so hard she sloshed her brew onto her cup's saucer. Alexandra was extremely witty and had Anne not seen her husband frown at being made the brunt of one of Alexandra's jokes, then she probably would have encouraged the lady to continue with her jests. However, as much as she enjoyed the playful taunts, she was growing weary and was glad when Alexandra stopped her teasing.

Edward kept his eyes on his amused and expectant wife for he knew it was during the afternoon hours when she regularly fell into slumber. Today, was no exception. He watched her energy rapidly decline and like a door slamming shut, her heavy eyelids dropped suddenly. Only because he was watching her was he able to reach her side in time to catch her. His abrupt actions ceased the jovial parlour banter.

He announced to his gasping guests his countess needed a nap and to Lawrence's chagrin, Lady Deneham agreed a short repose would be just the thing to invigorate all the ladies. She looked at Meg and insisted she retire to her room, but when she went to address her niece, she found her absent. Lawrence had seen Alicia exit the parlour the minute she heard her aunt order Meg to her room. He was sure Alicia escaped to the stables, dreading the idea of sleeping the day away.

Simon and Lawrence were left to their own company when Felton and Sir Marcus went to visit the Marquis of Beaumont. Lawrence would have liked to slip away to rescue Meg from her confinement, but he thought Simon read his mind for the man refused to leave his company. He immediately engaged him in a discourse on archery. If Lawrence wasn't so single-mindedly thinking of Meg, he probably would have enjoyed the discussion offering him sound advice on how to improve his skill. He listened half-heartedly and as soon as he could, he feigned an excuse, took his leave and made his way to Meg's private suite. He hoped to convince her to walk with him in the garden and was prepared to argue fresh air was as invigorating as a short nap. He rapped softly on her bedroom door and was sorry when his tattoo went unanswered. Disappointed, he returned to the parlour, hoping Meg might have thought to seek him out.

He noticed the French doors leading to the knot garden were open and quickly made his way to see if Meg was there waiting for him. He found her sitting on a marble bench and was about to make his way to her until he saw Simon standing before her offering her a single daffodil. He heard Meg giggle and the sound of her laughter, soft and enchanting, characteristically annoyed him, but this time it was not because he thought she was mocking him. What bothered him was the source of her laughter. After all, he was sure it was not the first singular flower she had ever received.

Lawrence could not see Meg's face, but he was pretty sure Simon was enjoying one of her bright-eyed smiles and that disturbed him even more than the sweet laughter she gifted him. He ground his lips, disturbed that it was Simon and not himself wooing Meg. He turned on his heel and left, hissing under his breath, "Ha! A single stem, indeed!"

He called for the butler, Simmons, and ordered him to summon the head gardener. Within the half hour, Lawrence held a bouquet of flowers procured from the cutting garden that made Simon's gift of a single stem look paltry. He only hoped Meg still sat on the stone bench where he last saw her and Simon was no longer present.

Lawrence found Meg looking adorably sweet with her chocolate-brown hair shimmering with reddish highlights, holding her posture, her hands resting in her lap. He felt lucky to find her alone and walked up to greet her, but when he stood in front of her, he found her deep in thought with her eyes closed. He waited for her to notice him and when she continued to be unaware of his presence, he wondered what thoughts distracted her. He frowned when he considered Simon was the man keeping Meg's mind captive.

Feeling at peace for the first time in a while, Meg closed her eyes to reflect on her conversation with Simon. His romantic gesture of proffering her a single daffodil from behind his back with a gallant bow had made her smile. He was remarkably charming and why she never felt anything other than brotherly love for him, she would never be able to understand. She refused his suit, again, and Simon surprised her by not receiving her rejection with his normal good humor. It was clear to Meg, in that moment, her dearest friend had something momentous to announce. He professed nothing would make him happier than to make her his wife, but if he was not the man she would call husband, then she might be happy to know Lord Atwood did not repulse him. He grinned and Meg laughed. Meg admitted she did love the wretched viscount and Simon confessed he realized at the Davenport Ball she might have fallen for the man. Simon informed her both Beaumont and Felton regarded Atwood highly and her parents would approve of the match if that was her wish. Then, he reminded her how he needed to marry by his thirtieth birthday in order to comply with his grandmother's wishes to inherit her bequest. The land was his future and if indeed Meg was determined not to marry him, then he needed to return tomorrow to London to enter the *marriage mart*. He shuddered and Meg laughed again. She gave Simon her hopes he would find a lady more worthy than she, but Simon just scoffed at her remark. She begged him to stay at least one more day and he agreed.

"Meg?" Lawrence prompted. "Are you sleeping or *woolgathering*?"

Meg's eyes shot open. She laughed at seeing the viscount's brows scrunched up together, his lips tight in a scowl and wondered, *"What could be the matter with him now?"*

"My lord, I was quite at peace until I opened my eyes to find you frowning at me. Am I to blame for your ill humor?"

Lawrence relaxed his fretful features, his eyes widening as her words resonated. Lately, it seemed he wore his emotions for everyone to see and that disturbed him, "I am responsible for my own disposition, Meg, and if I appeared unsettled it is because I was not the first to present you with a token of esteem."

Meg looked confused, but upon following the direction of where Lawrence looked, she realized he was staring at the flower she held in her hand, the daffodil Simon gifted her, "Ah, my flower. Yes, it was a gift from Simon. He is most thoughtful."

"And brave. Morris, Beaumont's head gardener, will not be pleased to see his garden assaulted. The man has eagle eyes and will know he is missing a daffodil from one of his pristine flower beds."

Alarmed, Meg chided, "You will not tell, my lord. I would be most unhappy to be responsible for any hardship Simon received on my behalf."

"As you wish," he replied indifferently.

Meg watched Lawrence's face change from somber to mischievous, offering her an impish smile. He swept his hand from behind his back to present her with the collection of flowers he had kept hidden from her, "May I present a token of my own esteem to you, Meg?"

Lawrence was happy his offering surprised Meg and even more thrilled when she easily relinquished Simon's daffodil to the bench on which she sat. He transferred the thick bouquet of assorted flowers and ferns into her willing hands, feeling his face stretch with his growing smile, "It is only a small sign of my esteem, Meg, for I would have had to denude England of all its flowers to show you the depth of my feelings."

Meg laughed at his theatrical declaration and then she thanked him, exclaiming the flowers were beautiful. She inhaled their marvelous scent and returned Lawrence's smile. The resonating chime made her turn her head towards its source and reminded her it was time to dress for dinner. She turned back to excuse herself from Lawrence, "Mama will seek me out to learn if I heard the gong. She will not be happy to find me missing. I best take my leave of you, my lord, so that I might change."

"Never change, Meg."

Meg gasped an "O," before her eyes twinkled in understanding. Lawrence had just declared he liked her as is. She felt herself blush before she rose from her seat, dipped a curtsy and departed.

During dinner, the ladies re-instigated their teasing discourse regarding their win in the archery tournament which provoked the men to defend themselves earnestly. Their rebuttals sounded as if they were making testimony to a magistrate. Both Sir Marcus and Simon accused Felton of being in league with the women, to which, an affronted, but grinning Lawrence rebuked, "I am not a woman!"

Lady Deneham with affectation debated with her husband that she was the better archer, even though she had only tied him in their match. She proclaimed her skill was superior to his own since none of her arrows had shot wide. Sir Marcus shouted, "unfair" to a chuckling crowd and while he laughed, he took the white table linen from his lap and waved it in surrender, yielding to his wife's persuasive arguement. The friendly and teasing repartee continued until Lady Felton rose from the table to signal the women it was time to retire and leave the men to their port.

"I hope, my lord husband, you do not keep us waiting long for we are anxious to enjoy our winnings."

"Since it displeases me to see you anxious, Anne, you may expect us to join you sooner than later." Edward waited for the women to exit before he commanded his footman to bring the tray of glasses and port to him. He picked up the decanter and informed the head footman that he would see to his own guests, and waited until his footman dismissed and exited with the other servants, before he poured the sweet liquid into the crystal tumblers. As he handed the glasses over, he heard Sir Marcus ask, "Well, Atwood, do you know what will be required of us?"

"No, not I, sir. I may have been on the ladies' team, but they did not entrust me with their wishes."

"Nor I," exclaimed Simon.

Edward's silence brought his peers to look at him. Sir Marcus barked, "Well go on, my lord, what do they wish for us to do?"

"Not us," Edward looked at Simon, "our forfeit falls upon one in our group."

Simon's face colored from embarrassment, "They did not!"

"I am sorry, Ware, but it is their wish and you are honor-bound to comply."

Lawrence asked, "What am I missing? What must he do, and why are you and Sir Marcus excluded from doing it with him?"

Sir Marcus laughed when he reasoned their forfeit, “It seems Ware owns the burden of payment singularly. I, for one, have no musical talent of merit, so I cannot offer, even if I wanted to stand in his stead. What of you, Felton?”

Edward ginned and shook his head from side to side. Lawrence, not sure of the private joke that seemed to be amusing everyone, asked, “Would someone please enlighten me?”

“It seems, Atwood," answered Simon, "the Denehams, for whom I consider the most intimate of friends, have revealed to Lady Felton I have a hidden talent. I do not remark upon it because I play for my own pleasure and have no desire to become parlour entertainment. My talent is known to only a few and I would prefer to keep it that way. I ask that none of you reveal it in idle chatter.”

“I will not make sport of you, if that is what concerns you,” remarked Lawrence.

Edward interjected, “I do not believe that concerns him, Atwood. My wife is under the impression Ware is most accomplished.”

Simon shrugged his shoulders when Felton’s eyes fell on him, “Since I have not performed for a critical audience, who is to say?”

Edward finished his port and encouraged his guests to do so as well, "It is time, Gentlemen, to pay the piper."

The men entered the music room and Meg rushed to meet Simon with her sympathetic words, "Simon, you must know I had no hand in this. I know how much you loathe performing to an audience and I would never, being of the same mind, ask it of you. You must not fret, besides, you know you are more than capable."

Lady Deneham intervened, "Do not be mad at Meg, Simon. It was all my doing. Without thought, I remarked to Lady Felton how no one of our acquaintance played finer than you. She is desirous to hear you play and knowing you to be of a disposition to want to please your host, I suggested the forfeit."

"I do beg your pardon Mr. Ware," apologized Lady Felton. "I was unaware you would find the request abominable. I would not wish to make you ill at ease. I suggest ladies we choose another forfeit."

"Nonsense," replied Simon, "I am most happy to comply. It is true I do not perform publicly, so I will ask each of you to not remark upon this display of my ability to the *bon ton*. I do not relish being asked to entertain at every affair I attend. You know very well the leaders of our society are constantly on the prowl for discovering and showcasing new talent. Heaven help me, if Lady Jersey hears of this performance."

Lawrence watched Simon take his seat on the piano bench while Meg found a chair that gave Simon a view of her should he look up from the keyboard. It seemed to him Meg was offering Simon her support as though his performance was a trial to him. Her protective manner unsettled him. He was so busy observing the nuances between them he was the last to take a seat. The room hushed waiting in anticipation for Simon to begin. Lawrence saw him adjust his bench seat to a proper distance from the pianoforte, stretch his fingers, stroke the keyboard, and then carefully place his fingers on the ivory keys. It appeared when Simon closed his eyes he was preparing his body and soul for his performance. Everyone waited and then were surprised when Simon's staid fingers began to hit the keys with great enthusiasm.

Simon opened his first movement with a lively sixteenth note phrase. His fingers hit each ivory key with crispness and fluidity, bringing fullness to the piece by smoothly playing the tied arpeggios in the bass. Lawrence would have thought Simon was impervious to his surroundings if not for an occasional glance at Meg. He found himself completely mesmerized by Simon's performance, watching the man's fingers speed across the keys, repeating the phrase through changed harmonies and shifting key-centers. Simon finished the fifteen-minute sonata with a *scherzo*, a boisterous conclusion to the score. No sooner did his fingers still than Meg rose to congratulate him. The room immediately filled with resounding applause. Lawrence rose with the others and added to the cacophony with his own clapping hands. The noise reverberated until Simon acknowledged the praise with a bow.

Edward was the first to inquire, "The piece was Beethoven, Ware?"

"One of his earlier pieces. Sonata Number 10."

"They say he is completely deaf now," added Sir Marcus.

"And yet," offered Simon, "he is still composing. I am anxiously expecting the delivery of a new piece from his Vienna publisher Artaria. Critics boast it is one of his best works. They say he dedicated the piece to his friend the Archduke Rudolph."

Lady Felton moved to her husband's side and interrupted their discourse, "I am sorry I promised to keep this performance a secret, Mr. Ware. You have a rare talent that should be shared."

"Nay, Meg can perform with equal skill."

The comment hushed the room. The revelation brought all eyes upon Meg who exclaimed in horror, "No! Simon jests. I have never performed to an audience."

"That is indeed true, but, she has played for me and with me for years."

Lady Deneham guffawed, "Really, Simon. Are you telling me my daughter is accomplished and her papa and I know nothing of it? How can that be?"

"Well, my lady, it is as she wished. There were many times where the music you remarked upon escaping from the music room was not of my doing but hers. You see, your daughter and I are kindred spirits in the way we play. We perform to soothe our countenances, not our egos."

Sir Marcus asked, "Is this true, Meg?"

"Well, Papa, I have played for years with Simon. I thought nothing of my ability. Indeed, I cannot say I have any, since I have never formally taken a lesson."

"Well, then, how did you learn to play?" asked her mother.

"A prodigy?" suggested Edward.

Meg covered her mouth with her hand holding back her nervous laughter. Simon explained, "Meg has a natural talent; however, she has practiced long and hard with me. I am no easy taskmaster when it comes to the pianoforte."

"Well, Meg," commanded her father. "It is time, you enlightened us. Show us what you know."

"Please, Papa, may I defer until we are private? I am not prepared."

"Nonsense. If Simon speaks true, than you are more than prepared."

Meg looked to Simon for help, "It is only right, Meg, that we debut together."

"Then, together it shall be, Simon. You would not refuse to perform a duet with me."

Simon noted the glint in Meg's eyes telling him she was confident in his reply. He marveled at her cleverness to get him to share the spotlight with her. He bowed to her and escorted her back to the piano bench where they each took a seat side by side.

Lawrence watched their interplay and realized, by their obvious familiarity with one another, that they must have spent a great deal of time practicing together. They performed a popular piece by Handel, one he had heard at more than one musicale; and while the music was exceptional, Lawrence's thoughts distracted him from appreciating the piece. Lawrence thought Meg and Simon looked remarkable together and it soured his stomach to see them so well matched in their interests. It was obvious Simon held Meg's esteem and camaraderie. As he watched the pair, he convinced himself the reason Meg rejected his proposal was because of her love for Simon.

Nerves kept Meg from looking at Lawrence or anyone else in the audience. She was happy Simon chose a piece of music they had played enough times together that she was able to perform without thought. She would never have survived a solo performance without Simon by her side to calm her and offer his support. When the music ended, she dropped her head in embarrassment, assured she had not performed well, but Simon must have read her thoughts for he squeezed her hand and congratulated her on a job well-done. She responded to his praise with a smile and hoped Lawrence was of the same opinion.

Her mother exclaimed, "Well, Daughter, you are a wonder!"

Meg raised her head filled with pride over her mother's exclamation and searched out to see if Lawrence was in agreement. She found him frowning and though his scowl was becoming familiar to her, she wondered what was at the root of his concern this time. *Could it be her reluctant suitor was about to abandon her once again?* Rather than fall into despair, she decided to place her faith in him. After all, he had professed his love and intentions. Perhaps, his grimace was over her long-standing friendship with Simon.

After what seemed an odious amount of time discussing her hidden talent, everyone retired to the parlour where Lady Felton instructed her servants to set up one card table. Lord Felton and Sir Marcus had declined to play cards, opting instead for a game of billiards, so Anne and Alexandra, without partners, decided to sit near the recently stoked fire to chat quietly.

Both Meg and Alicia were surprised when Lawrence asked Alicia to be his partner at cards. Before Meg could ask Lawrence why he did not choose her, she heard Simon chuckle, "I see you already know who has the better hand at cards, Atwood."

Simon caught Meg's frown and added, "Do not fret, Meg, I have enough skill for the both of us to come about. You must not forget I know you well enough to read your mind and make the most of our play."

Meg smiled, knowing Simon's words to be true. When she turned to see if Lawrence thought his rebuke of her skill funny, she was sorry to see his temperament had not improved. By the conclusion of the second set, Meg decided she had endured enough of Lawrence's petulance and retired for the evening. She had tried her best to improve his mood by smiling brightly at him and contributing plenty of frivolous banter, but no matter her attempts at coquetry, she could not appease Lawrence's dark mood. Before long, she excused herself, complaining she had the headache and wished to retire to her room.

Alicia could not blame her cousin for taking her leave, for the cheerful camaraderie the small group enjoyed over dinner was gone. She decided she suffered the dismal party long enough as well, and bid the gentlemen good night before retiring to her own room. When Alicia departed, Simon raised an eyebrow at Lawrence and waited to see if the viscount would offer an explanation. He did not. Instead, he left Simon's company to bid his hostess and the observant Lady Deneham good evening, before making his way to his room.

Chapter Seventeen

Lawrence woke later than usual the next day after enduring a troubled night. Sometime as dawn approached, his jealousy of Meg's and Simon's friendship abated, but then his regrets over his surly mood kept him from sleep. The only thing that finally relaxed him into slumber was the hope Meg would give him the opportunity to apologize for his ungentlemanly behavior.

Entering the breakfast room, he was disappointed to see the house party, minus Lady Felton and Lady Deneham, finishing up their morning meal. He took note of Simon's, Alicia's, and Meg's riding dress and deduced the hour was later than he thought if they had already taken their morning ride. Meg looked exhausted and he cursed himself, knowing he was the reason for her disheartened state, especially when she turned her attention to her meal the moment he entered the room, "Good morning. I see I am late to rise and have missed accompanying you on your morning jaunt."

Lawrence's friendly greeting caused Meg to lift her head and look at him. *"He is no longer ill-tempered,"* she mused and then wondered why she cared an iota for this lord whose mood vacillated between surliness and pleasantry.

She might have discerned the message behind his pleading eyes if her father's voice had not interrupted their gaze, "We must take our leave tomorrow, Felton. My wife wishes to attend the Riverton Masquerade Ball. She will not disappoint her hosts for they are longtime friends. I will be sorry to take your leave."

Before Lord Felton could respond, Simon added, "I must depart tomorrow as well, my lord. I thank you for tolerating my company."

"You are very tolerable, Ware," chuckled Edward, "and may own an open invitation anytime you wish to visit."

Simon smiled and thanked the earl who had earned his respect and friendship.

Meg was surprised by her father's announcement for her parents had not apprised her of their plans to leave. Before she could make an inquiry, she heard Lawrence ask her father, "Will Miss Alicia Deneham and your daughter take their leave as well, Sir Marcus?"

Lawrence cast his eyes on Meg's father and wondered the real reason behind the Deneham's departure. While Sir Marcus and Lady Deneham agreed to support his suit, he knew it was conditional on Meg's happiness. He remembered Sir Marcus's exact words: *"We shall stay as long as I believe my daughter's happiness requires you in it."* No doubt, Sir Marcus saw his daughter's solemn and circumspect mood this morning and guessed his inconstant attentions were at the root of Meg's sadness. Sir Marcus probably wanted to remove Meg from him as quickly as possible.

As much as Sir Marcus wanted to protect his daughter from the lord that seemed to distress her beyond all proportions, he knew Meg was the only one who could decide what made her happy. He left the decision, to stay or go, to her, so with restraint he answered, "That is for them to determine, Atwood. Lady Felton remains amenable to having guests, so I will let the girls decide what they wish to do." Sir Marcus then took his leave and exited the breakfast parlour.

Alicia announced, "We shall decide later. For now, let us finish our plans for today. Simon suggested an excursion and we have agreed to picnic at Kenilworth. Do you join us, Lord Atwood?"

"Definitely." Deserving or not of the invitation, he would not refuse the opportunity to spend time with Meg. He was sorry he was the cause behind the heavy tension weighing upon them and realized that he must be frowning again when Meg's expression faltered, as though he had spoken a harsh word to her. He almost cursed aloud for wearing his feelings in clear sight of everyone's scrutiny. *Could she not see his anger was only with himself?*

Lord Felton loaned his guests two sporting curricles and a wagon carrying four servants with all the food and accoutrements necessary for a pastoral picnic. The full wagon left before the party departed, with instructions for the servants to set up the picnic on Kenilworth's tiltyard, the grassy lawn area once used in medieval times for jousting. The attending servants would serve the young party when it arrived.

Over the years, the ruined medieval castle was a recommended attraction for travelers interested in significant architectural and historical locations, but as word spread among the grapevine that Sir Walter Scott was working on a novel with Kenilworth as it's backdrop, picnicking at the castle ruins quickly became popular. Constructed over several centuries from Norman through Tudor times, the historical castle was reputed to have been one of England's strongholds, withstanding the longest siege, six months, in English history. Over centuries, the semi-royal castle was enlarged and fortified to withstand assaults from land and water and only fell when Parliament in 1649 destroyed it to prevent it from being used as a military stronghold in England's civil war. Only two buildings remained habitable.

Lawrence helped Meg into the lead curricle while Simon saw to assisting Alicia in the second carriage. They had changed from their riding habits into fashionable walking dresses and he could not help but note how fetching Meg looked in her lemon-colored *gros de Naples* pelisse and large bonnet of gossamer satin. The collar, wrists, and hem of her pelisse were all trimmed with two narrow fluted full flounces and by the way she primped at them, Lawrence guessed her pelisse and hat were new. He quickly offered her a compliment, but her weary eyes told him she was chary of his good humor. He wished he could explain his surly behavior from the night before without admitting he was jealous of her relationship with Simon, though he knew he would have no choice but to confess his envy, if she would not forgive him.

As he made his way around to the driver's side of the curricle, his thoughts were so distracting that he did not see Simon alight himself to sit next to Meg. He would have jumped up into the man's lap if Simon had not remarked, "You don't mind? Do you, Atwood? I have a few things to discuss with Meg and since I depart tomorrow, I thought the ride was my best chance of having an uninterrupted discussion with her."

"Precisely," thought Lawrence, *"for that was my intention."* He wanted to swear, *"Bloody Hell,"* and tell the usurper to remove himself promptly, but decorum forced him to relinquish his seat with courtesy.

Lawrence made his bow to Meg before moving to take his seat in the second curricle. Alicia was already seated and waiting for him to take his place next to her. He thought she offered a conciliatory smile. As soon as he had the reins in hand, he gave his *tiger* the command to release the matching bays' heads. The small groomsman quickly jumped up and took his station at the back of the curricle, where he would stand until he was needed to care for the horses when they reached their destination. Lawrence gently slapped the leather straps and within seconds, he maneuvered his team in tandem with Simon's curricle.

"Meg? You are not angry with me for taking Atwood's seat, are you?"

"It was rather mischievous of you, Simon. It was obvious he wished to drive me."

"Well, he has put you out of sorts on more than one occasion. A bit of his own medicine, will not hurt the fool one iota."

"Do not abuse him, Simon. It is ill-mannered of you to do so, and I take great offense. I care for you deeply and it would grieve me terribly if you did not respect Lord Atwood. He truly is an honorable man, even if at times he acts. . ." Meg paused thinking how to finish her comment and then reluctantly added, "without thought."

Simon laughed with much gusto and Meg cringed, "Admit it, Meg, you wanted to say abominably."

Meg smiled, "Well, he was rather surly last night, but I am sure he had his reasons. He is a sensitive man and I do not mean emotional, but caring. I feel any reluctance on his part is because he feels deeply for me."

"How can you be sure?"

"Because, I feel a similar confusion regarding him."

"What are you confused about, Meg?"

"I do not know if we are truly suited, Simon. I seem to rile him at every turn."

"Perhaps, you should rethink my proposal, Meg. We are well-suited and I know we would never discommode each other. You would be content with me."

"I know I would, Simon. A life with you would be very pleasant." Meg paused and then continued, "You once told me we do not choose love, but that it chooses us. I am smitten, Simon, and have no choice but to follow my heart. You will thank me one day when you find your own *love match*."

"Is it love that defeats me then?"

"Only a *love match* could make me accept an offer other than yours."

"Then, I take no offense, Meg, for my desire is to see you happy."

Meg smiled, "Thank you, Simon. You must know I wish to see you happy, too."

"Do not thank me yet, Meg, for I confess I will not give way to your Lord Atwood until he has proven his mettle with me."

"You are frowning again, my lord," stated Alicia.

"I beg your pardon, Miss Deneham," replied Lawrence. "But I find it hard not to do so, when I spy such a happy couple before me. Do you think she has relented and accepted Ware's offer?"

"Don't be a fool, my lord. Do you think Meg fickle? She is not the one that shifts hot and cold like the flip of a coin. Meg is nothing but constant in her affection. I do not think you can say the same."

"Not true! My love for your cousin is constant. It is my confidence that is lacking."

"Do you trust Meg? If you do then you should be self-assured and not jealous of a long-standing friendship. If you want Meg, then offer for her."

"I did and she refused."

"Impossible. I know she considers no one else but you."

"She demands a courtship."

"Then, I suggest, my lord, you court her and forget about any other suitor. Your success depends entirely on you and you alone."

Chapter Eighteen

The small party approached the red sandstone ruins of Kenilworth Castle from the tiltyard, where on a grassy knoll the 12th century great Norman tower, with its huge corner turrets, is prominently seen standing one hundred feet tall. A number of picnickers covered the verdant lawn and a band of Elizabethan costumed performers meandered among the crowd soliciting coin for their act. It was common to see a traveling troupe making its way to Avon-upon-Stratford, William Shakespeare's birthplace, to put on a show by informally setting up a stage area using the Kenilworth ruins for a backdrop. Now that the castle was attracting tourists, these traveling actors found it easy to earn some currency from the gentry and aristocracy visiting the popular site.

Lawrence followed Simon onto the causeway and took care to maneuver his team among the multiple conveyances crowding the lane. As he waited to move his curricle forward, he searched the festive landscape for

Beaumont's standard where his servants would be waiting to serve them their noon meal. He soon found the pennant snapping, battling the forceful wind, apprising him how quickly the weather had altered since their departure from Beaumont Manor. The day had been warm and mild when they started their journey, but now a brisk coolness greeted them. He hoped they would be able to complete their excursion before England's erratic climate intruded.

Lawrence brought his team to a halt and waited for his *tiger* to jump down to take hold of his horses' bridles, so he could help Alicia to debark. When Alicia was clear of the curricle, Lawrence changed places with his *tiger* to hold the horses from running off until his groomsman controlled them with the reins from the driver's seat. Once Lawrence saw his *tiger* had his cattle firm in hand, he released the horses' bridles and watched his groomsman maneuver the curricle over to a location designated for visiting equipages. Only then, did he turn and join Alicia. He immediately searched out Meg and saw her smile at him when he found her. He marveled at how she could transform his disposition with a mere grin. He stood transfixed looking at her until Simon proffered his arm to escort Meg away.

Alicia shook her head and grabbed Lawrence's arm to follow them. She thought it ridiculous how two people who clearly admired one another should have such a difficult time getting together. While it was true Simon's attentions were proving irksome, she believed Lawrence only needed to assert himself in order to thwart Simon's interference.

Beaumont's staff were ready to serve them with the accoutrements and foods for a grand affair laid out for them to partake. Lawrence was still not used to the pomp and circumstance of his station and felt awkward at having so much food placed for his personal consumption. It bothered him to know most of the food would be repacked and returned, perhaps even thrown away. He cringed at the waste, remembering how many of England's countrymen had little or nothing to eat. He much preferred the small meal they enjoyed the day they went riding. Regardless of his preferences, he understood this show of wealth was the way of nobility and that he would be expected to present a similar fare when he hosted or else be marked a miser by the *ton*.

Lawrence watched Simon assist Meg onto the Aubusson carpet blanketing the lawn for their picnic. Simon then placed a decorative pillow behind Meg to support her back, before flipping his coattails to sit beside her. Lawrence noted Meg's appeasing smile and hoped it meant she was not happy with Simon's proprietary behavior. He followed Simon's lead and helped Alicia with her seating and then sat next to her. His eyes never left Meg, though he watched her surreptitiously. His heart raced a tad faster when she found him looking at her. He did not know how long they held each other's gaze, but the moment broke when Beaumont's footman offered a tray holding goblets of wine. They each took a glass and Simon offered a toast, "To the beauty that surrounds us."

Lawrence was not fooled to think Simon's remark referred to the landscape. Simon's gaze upon Meg and her crimsoned blush made it evident his compliment was intended for one person only and it galled Lawrence. He watched while Simon picked up a bowl of strawberries with his free hand to offer the delicacy to Meg. A multitude of bowls were placed around them containing fresh fruit, spiced nuts, and macaroon cookies. Lawrence was only marginally ameliorated when Meg refused Simon's offer. The somber group watched each other carefully until Alicia broke the awkward silence for which Lawrence was grateful, "It is amazing how this set of ruins has recently attracted so many visitors considering England is full of decrepit and ruined castles. I expect it is Scott who is responsible for Kenilworth's popularity."

Simon agreed, "Indeed, his novels are widely read and this new endeavor of his regarding the alleged murder of Amy Robsart, the first wife of the Earl of Leicester during our Virgin Queen's reign, is expected to be well-received."

"The murder mystery will definitely draw readers," added Lawrence, "but I believe the historical elements will be the substance for Scott's success. He is an ardent researcher. The pageantry Robert Dudley presented for Queen Elizabeth during her visit in July of 1575 is one of the reasons Kenilworth is of historical significance. It is said the queen's entourage numbered over several hundred and that the earl nearly went bankrupt to entertain her."

"Ah, yes," remarked Simon, "the fireworks and the lavish displays on the mere with the legendary Lady of the Lake attending her nymphs."

"You have read Robert Laneham's account of the queen's entertainment?" asked Lawrence.

Simon raised an eyebrow, but before he could answer, Meg exclaimed, "Oh, look! The troupe is performing!"

Everyone turned to look at the small group of Elizabethan actors exaggerating their performance in order to entertain the lawn guests who most likely were unable to hear their dialogue. Lawrence recognized the play immediately as the one he saw with Meg at the Theatre Royal. The costumes of the King and Queen of the Fairies were notable, but it was the impish character Puck that clearly identified the play to him. He looked at Meg to see if she recognized the scene they were performing and realized she had the moment he caught her eyes, "Would you like to move closer to hear the play?"

Simon's interruption kept Meg from answering, "It would be rude of us to leave this feast without partaking, Atwood. I am sure the ladies are famished and Felton's staff must be weary waiting to serve us. Let us finish our meal and then send them back to Beaumont Manor before we embark on any adventure."

With a smirk, Alicia remarked, "How thoroughly common, Simon, to concern yourself with the helps' discomfort."

Meg smiled at Simon. She knew her cousin was being facetious, but felt she needed to come to her neighbor and lifelong friend's defense, "But very much like him to think of others."

Lawrence noticed Simon's face flush at Meg's compliment and before he could overanalyze Meg's motivation to come to Simon's aid, she turned to him, "Not unlike you, my lord. You are also very considerate."

Lawrence beamed from her compliment and then blushed for feeling like a school boy having received his first accolade for a job well-done. Before he could respond, Alicia exclaimed, "What! Am I not worthy of praise, Cousin? Am I to believe that you find me lacking in consideration?"

Alicia's outburst erupted an unexpected guffaw from Meg whose blush brought chuckles from Simon and Lawrence. She quickly sobered and complimented her cousin, "My dear Alicia, you are all that I could ask for in a cousin, considerate and more."

Well-satisfied with herself for making everyone laugh, Alicia raised her goblet to be refreshed by the hovering footman and toasted, "To our considerate noblemen, may their modest numbers grow."

"Here, here," the group cheered. The high-spirited mood continued while they enjoyed their picnic of roasted pheasant, wafer thin sliced ham, a variety of sweetmeats, pies, cheeses, and fruits. They compared the Regent's fete honoring Lord Wellington with the Earl of Leceister's entertainment for Queen Elizabeth, remarking upon the costs associated with hosting the incomparable festivities. "Nothing," they agreed, "could have been more of a spectacle than the reenactment of the Battle of Trafalgar on the Serpentine to celebrate England's victory over France. Meg noticed that both gentlemen kept the conversation light, even though she was sure they held strong opinions on how the Prince Regent continually dipped into the realm's treasury as if it was his private bank account. She was also aware of how attentive Lawrence was to her needs. When her goblet was low with wine, he called to have the footman refill it. When she was about to reach for a spiced nut, she found Lawrence anticipating her desire and handed her the plate. When an urchin selling a bunch of posies approached their party, he purchased two bouquets, one for her and one for Alicia. Then, comprehension dawned and she understood that Lawrence was courting her.

"I, for one, am ready to stretch my legs and take a look at these grounds," announced Alicia. "I am surprised Lord Clarendon does not mind having so many trespassers on his property."

"He only uses the land for farming," explained Simon. "I am sure the crowd we see today is uncommon and trespassers cause little problem for the earl. We just need to stay away from the gatehouse where the steward for this property resides."

Simon stood and helped Meg to her feet while Lawrence assisted Alicia to rise. Lawrence listened along with Meg as Alicia asked Simon a question regarding Kenilworth's towers. While Simon pointed out and began a discourse about the multi-sided Oriel Tower constructed by John of Gaunt in the 14th century, Lawrence swiftly took Meg's hand and pulled her away. He had no qualms taking advantage of Simon's distraction. He desired Meg's company and felt rather delighted at his quick thinking. They were a good hundred yards away, before he glanced over his shoulder. Simon was standing with arms akimbo, looking quite displeased with their departure. Lawrence could tell Alicia was doing her best to assuage his anger. His guilt surfaced and he looked to see if Meg wished to return to Simon's company, but when he saw her stifle a giggle, any remorse he had vanished in her bemusement. If she was not about to chide his actions, then neither would he.

They walked across the tiltyard that once acted as a dam for the mere, a great lake covering around a hundred acres. They made their way through the inner court and did not speak until they entered the ruins of the Great Hall, another of Gaunt's additions. Lawrence felt their thoughts were of equal solicitude and found comfort in that they could be content with one another without idle chatter.

"I have been wanting to make my apology to you for behaving badly last night, Meg. There is no excuse for it other than to say I let myself believe for one moment

Simon made a better match for you than me, which is why I was in such a foul mood. While my mind considered the idea, my heart would not accept it and the result was I was an intolerable and rude companion. I will not doubt us again, Meg. I love you and hope you will forgive me. "

Overcome with joy, Meg forgot herself and threw her arms around Lawrence's waist, pressing her head against his chest. She felt his arms circle her and embrace her. When her emotions calmed, she began to hear Lawrence's heartbeat and she took comfort in hearing the elevated rhythm. She turned her face up to look at the man she loved, "I can hear your heart beating."

Lawrence grinned and professed, "It only beats for you."

Meg laughed and felt giddy, but quickly sobered when she realized a number of people were looking at them. Embarrassed, she pushed at Lawrence's chest to gain a proper distance from him, but realized she could not budge him unless he wished it. Lawrence felt Meg's withdrawal and almost chuckled when he saw the audience their ardent embrace was drawing. He released her, but not before he placed a kiss on her forehead, "You give me leave to ask your parents for consent to pay my addresses?"

Meg couldn't stop grinning. She gave her consent happily.

Lawrence knew without a doubt they would be happy. Not because he was titled and held property or because she would bring a tidy sum to their union, but because they were in love and even as importantly, they believed in each other.

"Atwood!" called Simon. Both Lawrence and Meg turned to face Simon approaching with Alicia at his heels. He looked sober and Lawrence felt for Meg's ardent suitor.

"The wind is picking up. If you and Meg are finished here, I suggest we return to the manor. I do not think it will rain, but our climate is unpredictable at best. Besides, with this weather I am sure our teams are anxiously biting their bits."

Hastily, they left the Great Hall ruins and entered the inner court where a young woman distracted Meg's attention. The woman's behavior seemed erratic, as if she could not make up her mind on which direction she wished to pursue. One moment she seemed to be headed towards the outer courtyard, the next instant she retraced her steps and headed back towards the castle. Meg was so captivated by the woman's movements, that not until Lawrence asked her if she was ill, did she realize she had stopped walking, causing her party to question her behavior.

"I am fine, my lord. I am not sure I can say the same for that lady." Meg directed, with a tilt of her head, Lawrence's gaze to the woman in question, "Does she not seem frantic to you?"

"Oh, my!" exclaimed Lawrence as he pulled a surprised Meg in the direction of the young woman. It was not until she heard Lawrence call out her name that she realized Lawrence was acquainted with a Miss Wainscoat.

"Oh, Lord Atwood, never have I been so happy to see someone known to me."

"Surely, you are not alone."

"I fear I may be."

Meg tugged on Lawrence's elbow in case he had forgotten about his hovering and curious party, "Oh, do forgive me, Miss Deneham. May I introduce Miss Julia Wainscoat of Bedworth to you? Miss Wainscoat, I present Miss Margaret Deneham, The Honorable Alicia Deneham, and Mr. Simon Ware."

Each lady made a small curtsey and Simon extended the customary response of a gentlemanly bow. Once the introductions were made, Lawrence asked, "Where is your party, Julia?"

Meg was not sure she liked Lawrence on such friendly terms with this young and comely woman. Julia was of Meg's size, but unlike Meg whose features fell on the dark side, Julia owned glossy blond locks and cornflower blue eyes that appeared brighter from the blue trimmed pelisse she wore. In her anxious state, she looked vulnerable and Meg understood why Lawrence or any man, would come to Miss Wainscoat's aid.

Wide-eyed, Julia replied, "Oh Lawrence, I could tell Papa was not feeling well. He would not let us depart until he informed the other members of our party, the Fairfields, that we were leaving. He kept clutching his chest as though out of breath. All I could think to hasten him to leave was to assure him I would seek out the Fairfields whom managed to separate from us when I dallied in the Great Hall. I told him I would find them, inform them he had left, and return home with them. I grew concerned when he did not argue with me and immediately helped him back to our carriage with orders to our coachman to see him home. I don't even think he realized what I had done. I have been searching for the Fairfields, but," Julia bit her lower lip, trying to keep from crying, "I fear they have also departed. I cannot find them and until you came along, I was not sure what I was going to do."

Lawrence took his free hand and squeezed one of Julia's, "Your father must have been quite ill to agree to your suggestion, but do not fret, Julia. I will either find the members of your party or I will see you home myself."

Simon volunteered, "I would be happy to see the young lady home, if you will see to our own company, Atwood."

Meg knew Simon offered for her sake and was a little disappointed when Lawrence refused his gesture. Lawrence saw the fear in Julia's eyes, "Thank you, Ware, but the honor is mine. I know I can trust you to see to the safe return of the Miss Denehams." He then turned to Meg and whispered, "I will see you as soon as possible. I am anxious to speak with your father. Know there is no place I would rather be than with you."

Meg smiled and though she was disappointed in leaving Lawrence's company, she knew his gallantry was one of the facets she found most appealing about him.

"Very well, Atwood," said Simon. "I will inform your *tiger* of your intentions before we leave. We will see you at dinner then."

"Indeed." In a lower voice for only Meg to hear, he whispered, "I will be thinking of you."

Meg grinned, happy to have Lawrence's sweet words keep her company on her return trip to Beaumont Manor. She walked away with Simon and Alicia, leaving Lawrence with the fetching Julia to search for her neighbors.

Meg, Alicia, and Simon squeezed their bodies together to fit into the curricle designed for two passengers. Meg was glad of the tight fit for the unexpected change of weather created a harsh wind that was cutting across her face and neck with brutal force. She was sure both she and Alicia would require a balm to soothe their damaged windburned skins.

"I am sorry I did not think to use Beaumont's traveling carriage, instead of this open curricle," apologized Simon. "You both must be miserable. I do not even have a blanket to offer for you."

"You need not apologize, Simon," replied Meg. "The day started out perfectly fine. You may control many things; however, the weather is not one of them."

"Who is this woman Julia Wainscoat?" asked Alicia. "I have not heard of the family name, have you?"

"Not I," replied Simon.

"Nor I," agreed Meg.

Simon was about to remark upon Lawrence, but Meg could read his mind and cut his speech off before he could begin. She raised her hand and chastised, "Simon, do not! Lawrence did what was proper. He could not in good conscious entrust you, a complete stranger, to see her home. You must have seen how frightened she became at your offer. I expect she is newly out of the school room, though her figure is quite endowed for a woman her age."

Simon exclaimed with a laugh, "Meg! How thoroughly vulgar of you."

"Hardly, I am sure you did not miss that the young woman in question is remarkably beautiful and full-figured."

"Are you jealous, Meg?" asked Alicia.

"Perhaps a little. I cannot remember any gentleman ever coming to my rescue."

"Then, your memory is short indeed, for I recall a certain gentleman taking great offense to a man bumping into you at Cheapside."

"Oh, Alicia! How you are right. Lord Atwood is quite the knight in shining armor. A prince among princes."

Simon shouted, "Stop! You are making me ill. Must I remind you, Meg, you once thought I was your most gallant of suitors."

"Simon," consoled Meg. "I will always hold you in the highest esteem and love you always."

"Yes, but as you once told me, it is Atwood that holds your heart."

Meg smiled. She knew she needed to make no reply.

"Is it a done then, Meg?" asked Simon. "Am I to expect an announcement in the paper?"

"He is to speak to my parents after dinner, but yes, I have assured him of my answer."

"Are you happy, Meg?"

"Yes, Simon, very."

"Then, you have my felicitations."

"Mine too," added Alicia.

Meg replied with the joy that had filled her since the moment Lawrence professed his love. She cheerfully replied, "Thank you," and then spent the rest of the time daydreaming over her future with Lawrence while Simon and Alicia chatted. She was so excited with plans for her life she fairly leaped from the curricle when they reached Beaumont's manor home. She rushed up the front steps, through the door, up the main staircase, practically running to her mother's private suite, where she knew she would be napping, to tell her Lord Atwood had indeed come up to scratch and would seek a private conference with her father after dinner.

"Mama!" she called when she entered her mother's bedroom. Lady Deneham lay on her back on her quilted counterpane with a mask covering her eyes. She abruptly sat up when she heard her daughter's voice and pushed her eye mask up her forehead. With heavy eyes, she scanned her bedroom, waiting to see if Meg appeared or whether she conjured her daughter's voice from a dream.

Meg rushed and launched herself on her mother's mattress causing Lady Deneham to squeak at her daughter's youthful display, an act she had not witnessed since before she left the schoolroom. She reproved, "What is it, Meg, that has turned you into a graceless hoyden?"

"Oh, Mama! Lawrence loves me and I him. I am simply happy."

"He is speaking with your papa?"

"He plans to ask for permission after dinner, Mama. He had to assist a young lady first."

Lady Deneham pushed her mask off her head and pulled herself up to a proper sit. She was not sure she heard her daughter correctly and asked with a raised eyebrow, "He is what?"

"Oh, Mama! Do not look so alarmed. We came across a young woman of his acquaintance who became stranded. He felt duty-bound to see her safely home."

"Was she not chaperoned?"

"There was a miscommunication. Somehow her parties thought she was in the care of the other."

"What is this woman's name, Meg?"

"Julia Wainscoat. Do you know the family?"

"Not I, but perhaps our hosts do since most of Atwood's acquaintances were made through them when he came upon his title."

"Please do not look concerned, Mama," beseeched Meg. "There is nothing between this woman and Lawrence. The idea is absurd."

"We shall see."

Meg retired early. Her head was pounding. She realized she was probably hungry, but her appetite left her when Lawrence failed to appear for dinner. She discovered over her untouched meal that Lord Atwood and Julia Wainscoat met when he toured the Mediterranean with the Marquis of Beaumont. Her father, Sir Reginald Wainscoat, was a scholar and his well-read, articulate, and accommodating daughter, acted as an assistant to him during his travels. She further learned Lawrence and Julia bonded over their literary interests and enjoyed many evenings reading together and sharing opinions. Meg felt awkward, knowing Lawrence's absence, would be seen as another example of his reluctant suit. She knew if Lawrence failed to return by the morning, she would be required to leave with her parents when they returned to London. Even if she wanted to stay, Alicia's own departure made an extended visit impossible. She could not ask her hostess, who was ready to deliver her child within weeks, to be burdened with a guest that had no one to keep her company except herself. She was sorry her cousin needed to return to her own country home, but understood Alicia wanted to be present after receiving word her best mare was ready to foal. She prayed Lawrence was not in peril for she could think of no other reason that kept him from her side. She did not doubt his love. In that she was confident, but his past behavior made it difficult to convince her parents his offer was indeed sincere.

Her headache grew as the evening progressed. Her parents ranted over the viscount's absence. Sir Marcus criticized, "There is no excuse for not sending a message to you, Meg. He knew of your expectations and if his behavior is indicative of how he will treat you in the future, then you are better off without him. Simon would never be so thoughtless. Nothing would make him happier than for you to accept his offer."

"Stop, Papa! I care too much for Simon to marry him when I am in love with another man. He deserves better. Besides, I trust Lawrence. There is a reasonable explanation for his tardiness."

"Tardiness, indeed," mimicked Sir Marcus. "We leave tomorrow, Meg, whether Atwood returns or not."

Meg knew there was no arguing with her father and retired to her room. She hoped in the morning she would receive word from Lawrence informing her that he was well and indeed anxious to pay his addresses to her.

Chapter Nineteen

A day passed and still no message arrived from Lawrence. Meg was beside herself with worry and disappointment. Yesterday's ride home had been torture having to listen to her parents rant over Lord Atwood's ill treatment of their daughter. When she saw it was pointless to try to defend her suitor, she finally rested her head against the side of the carriage and feigned sleep, holding back the sobs that wanted to bubble forth in small bursts each time she heard one of her parents disparage her viscount. "I cannot believe my judgment was so wrong," professed Sir Marcus. "I was sure his intentions were sincere and his feelings profound."

No sooner did Meg alight from their traveling carriage than she retreated to her room, only leaving her private suite to learn if a letter arrived for her. She was confident Lawrence would dispatch a message explaining all and she waited anxiously to receive word from him. Her distress wearied her and annoyed her butler who, on more than one occasion, explained if a dispatch was delivered for her then she would already have it in her possession. By the time she had to ready herself for the Riverton Masquerade Ball she was completely exhausted.

Meg sat in front of her cheval glass mirror looking at her own and her maid's reflection while Mary pressed her hair into curls for the evening's ball. She thought she made a pathetic picture for a supposed shining debutante and faintheartedly listened when her maid gave her counsel, "Don't fret, miss, he won't disappoint you. Not that one. Don't forget he was not raised as a noble gent. I don't think he knows how to be anything he is not."

Meg's face brightened at the wisdom of her maid's advice and she resolved not to lose faith in Lawrence. She knew Mary's words spoke the truth. As much as Lawrence tried to own the hauteur of a nobleman, when it came to her, she knew he wore his feelings openly. Looking back, she realized all his scowls towards her were a result of how much she affected him, not disdainfully but ardently. There was no other explanation for her eliciting such a strong emotion from him unless he was attracted to her from the onset. Reason dictated that in the beginning if he disliked her, then he would never have sought her company or come to her aid. He professed he loved her and she would not let anyone, her parents or her own insecurities, sway her from believing in him. Feeling revived, she took a deep breath and straightened her posture. She told her maid, "I will not wear the shepherdess costume, Mary. Pray, bring me Hermia's dress."

Mary grinned, "Very good, miss."

Meg felt vulnerable dressed in Hermia's burgundy velveteen costume. It seemed everyone's eyes were upon her waiting to see if her Lysander would present himself. She shivered knowing her joy or heartbreak would be bantered about in tomorrow's parlours. She was sure everyone knew she admired Viscount Atwood and the realization made her a bundle of nerves. She felt her mother squeeze her hand in support after she exhaled a long breath. Her mother's touch reassured her and she felt better, especially having her mother and father standing by her side like two sentries.

She surprised her parents by presenting herself in their parlour wearing Hermia's costume. Lady Deneham raised an eyebrow at her daughter having remembered Lord Atwood dressed as Lysander at the last masquerade they attended. She was quick to deduce her daughter was the culprit behind securing the costumes from the Theatre Royal for them to wear, "So, Daughter, your mind is made up?"

Sir Marcus asked, "Her mind is made up about what, Alexandra?"

Meg explained, "Please, Mama, Papa. Give Lord Atwood a chance to show he is indeed worthy of me. I know he will not fail." She gave a cheeky grin and added, "He loves me and I him."

Sir Marcus shook his head, downhearted his precious daughter was doomed for heartbreak. His wife went forward and took her daughter's hand in her own, "Our greatest wish is for your happiness, Meg. If it lies with Viscount Atwood and he offers for you, we will not refuse his suit."

"Papa?"

Sir Marcus walked forward to assure his daughter he also desired her happiness, "It is as your mama professes. I will allow his lordship to pay his addresses to you if that is what you wish."

Meg smoothed her hands down her plush soft skirt. She felt pretty in her Elizabethan dress even though the velveteen, crisscrossed gold cord, and lace-trimmed stiff bodice flattened her bosom. She was used to the high-waist fashion of the day where she displayed to advantage her décolletage. Regardless, she felt absurdly regal in her Elizabethan dress.

She traced the gold cord crisscrossing halfway down her arm disappearing into a lace frill at her wrist and smiled at the exquisite detailing. The sleeves were tight fitted and puffed at her shoulders. The padded farthingale made her waist look very small and her hips full, reminding her of the full hoop formal skirts the queen required her subjects to wear when they were presented at court.

The waiting became unbearable causing Meg to doubt Lawrence and then she reminded herself how he had sought her out at the Davenport Ball against her father's wishes. He had said he did not want to disappoint her when she asked him why he had come. She knew he would not disappoint her this evening either. She quietly chanted, "He will come."

"What did you say, Meg?" asked her mother.

Meg did not realize she whispered the words aloud until she spied her mother's sorrow. She could not deal with her sympathy. She had her own emotions to contend with and needed a place of retreat to calm her wretchedly beating heart; otherwise, she feared she might swoon. Never before had her nerves peaked to such a level. She was sure if her mother touched her now, she would scream so loud the chandeliers above would quiver.

"Excuse me, Mama, but I need to make my way to the retiring room."

"Would you like me to attend you, Meg?"

"No, thank you. Really, I am fine. You should seek out Lady Riverton and Papa should make his way to the card room. Do implore him. You both have guarded me for long enough and I am simply weary of standing idly. I plan to seek out my friends. For a moment, I forgot I had any."

Lady Deneham smiled and agreed, "You are surrounded by many who hold you in high esteem. Do not let one man question your worth."

Meg left her parents to their own devices and since she had no need for the retiring room, she decided to venture into the garden where a bit of fresh air would settle her anxious state. She needed to reassess. She had placed too much significance on this ball, deciding that Lawrence's attendance would determine whether or not they had a future together. As her reasoning returned, she began to consider the unfairness of it all. He was not privy to her thoughts and therefore, his absence could not justly reflect his feelings. He might be injured or have a legitimate explanation for his absence. If that were the case, he would be sorely disappointed to see her lack of constancy towards him. *Do I have such little faith in him? Should not love strengthen our resolve, when outside forces threaten to separate us?*

Love. She loved Lawrence. The affirmation calmed her and brought her focus back to her surroundings. Her thoughts had carried her deeper into the garden than she intended and when she saw the burning glow of a cheroot she balked. A man partially hidden behind a stout oak tree was smoking and his concealment scared her. He must have heard her approach for he came more clearly into her view and proffered an inelegant bow. He was unmasked and unknown to her, though his attire of a domino marked him a guest of the Riverton's Masquerade Ball. He cavalierly held his demi-mask in his hand and twirled it as he stepped towards her. Something in his overt manner scared her and she instinctively turned to make her way back to the ballroom.

"My lady," he called. "You are a sight for someone dearly in need of company."

His salutation prompted Meg out of habit to turn back to him. She immediately regretted her proper manner of conduct when she remembered she was alone with a stranger in a secluded area of the garden. A stranger who was inebriated and looking at her like a predator. While she could see the lights of the ballroom above the hedges and hear the lively music, she knew she was physically hidden from any onlooker who would normally check the man's behavior. She could scream, but either way, whether this man mauled her or not, a scandal would ensue. She chastised herself. She knew better than to walk unprotected without a chaperone. Such behavior was considered wanton and Society was never forgiving. They would shun her and spew gossip for nothing entertained the *bon ton* more than to bring a peer low. There would be no sympathies, only slander and she cringed at her stupidity for placing herself in a reckless predicament, but it was better to bring every member of Society to her aid than to let this villain place one hand on her.

Again, Meg tried to return to the safety of the ballroom, but she had barely taken a step when the drunken man grabbed her arm. She opened her mouth to scream, but her effort was blocked when he used his other hand to cover her mouth. She desperately shook her head from side to side to try to free her mouth and the scream he had smothered. She thought she had succeeded when his grip loosened on her arm, but then she realized his momentary release was so he could better secure his hold of her by encircling her waist and pulling her back into his body. She heard him laugh as if they were in some playful joust. Her heart palpitated to an intolerable beat. She feared she would swoon, but then she remembered her resolve to fight and frantically thrust her elbow into the man's stomach with all her strength. She felt his hands relax and could not believe herself so capable in self-defense. She dared not turn around to see the injury she caused, but meant to run as fast as she could. She took two steps before she felt him grab her again, this time by the wrist. She closed her eyes willing herself to be strong again. She took her free arm, fisted her hand and swung it around with all the force she could muster. Her attacker ducked and then she heard her name.

"Meg, it's me!"

Meg opened her eyes and was relieved to see it was a rescuer that had grabbed her, not the villain she feared. She exclaimed in relief, "You came!"

Lawrence, dressed as Lysander in a doublet and jerkin, wrapped Meg in his arms, "Of course, I came. When you were not at Beaumont's, I followed you directly to Town."

"But you sent no word. It was as if everything between us had been a dream."

Lawrence frowned because he understood why Meg might have doubted him, but nevertheless it bothered him.

“You are frowning, my lord.”

“Only because my past behavior has made you doubt me, Meg. Not because of anything you have done."

At that moment, the villain who had manhandled Meg began to make some noises. Meg noticed his sprawled body on the ground, “What did you do to him?”

“Nothing he did not deserve. What in the world were you doing out here with him?”

“I was not in his company, my lord. He came upon me and took extraordinary liberties with my person.” After a pause, her voice trembled and she added, “I am glad you came when you did.”

“I am sorry I did not return as expected, Meg, but when I brought Miss Wainscoat to her home, we learned her father had an apoplectic attack. I could not leave her alone until I knew she and her father would be all right and I could not send you a message to explain my absence at dinner because they had no servant to carry one. I thought about sending my tiger, but then I would be stranded and delayed even further until he returned to collect me. Later when I finally left, I was not on the road a quarter of an hour when my curricle broke down."

Lawrence balked at the concern he saw in Meg's eyes and had to remind himself to finish his story, "I left my tiger to watch the carriage while I made my way to the nearest town to find someone to haul it to be fixed. I managed to transport the curricle and my groom, but the blacksmith shop was closed by the time I arrived, so I couldn't get the cracked axle repaired until the next day. I followed after you when I discovered you were no longer at Beaumont's and only stopped at Felton's town home to change into Lysander's costume. I knew you would be at the Riverton Masquerade and my coming as Lysander would please you. While I am sorry I missed escorting you here, I am happy to say at least I arrived when you needed me the most."

"How did you know I was in the garden?"

"I spoke with your parents, who by the way have given me permission to pay my addresses to you. They were rather cold at first, but eventually accepted my apologies for causing you distress."

"But how did you know to come to the garden?"

"Your mother said you needed a moment to compose yourself, so I sought you out here. It is where I knew you would be."

"You know me so well, then?"

"Yes, as I hope you know me. You did not truly doubt me, did you, Meg?"

"Perhaps, a little. But I never doubted my love for you."

"Well then, let us remove all doubt. Lady Riverton has granted your father permission to announce our engagement to the *ton* and I am looking forward to our betrothal waltz."

"You have no doubts, my lord, that I am the wife you want to spend the rest of your life?"

"None whatsoever. What about you? Have you now become the reluctant one?"

"Never. You are my heart's desire."

"Then we are of one mind. Come, I want everyone to know you have consented to be my wife."

"Forgive me, my lord, but I do not remember being asked."

Lawrence raised his eyebrows in surprise, trying to keep his chuckles from bursting forth, "Really, do you not?"

Meg laughed, "Well, not with my parent's permission."

"Ah, then I shall rectify my gaffe." Lawrence captured both of Meg's hands and drew her close. Looking into her eyes, he professed, "I love you Meg. I cannot imagine spending my life without you. I want to share everything with you, even my frowns."

Meg laughed, but stifled her giggles so as not to distract Lawrence from proposing.

"I promise to love you, protect you, and cherish you. Will you please marry me?"

Meg responded with a beaming "yes." She willingly went into his arms to share a heartfelt kiss before returning to the ballroom where her parents and Lady Riverton awaited them. Lady Riverton was thrilled her ball would be made a success with Miss Deneham's surprising betrothal. She could hardly wait to recall the romantic overture when she made tomorrow's afternoon calls. No doubt she would give herself some credit for Miss Deneham securing the most eligible Viscount Atwood. Of course, she had no role, but only she knew that and no one would dare correct her, not even her good friend Lady Deneham, who she knew would allow her to have this little triumph. It would last only until the next scandal or when something else of significance occurred, but she would enjoy her success while she could.

Lady Riverton drew everyone's attention so Sir Marcus could announce the betrothal of his daughter to Viscount Atwood. The room was silenced by the revelation and then began to rumble as their peers exclaimed their congratulations. Meg and Lawrence smiled at having their union received so heartily and were soon bombarded by their friends. Ladies hugged Meg, while the gentlemen slapped Lawrence's shoulder and shook his hand. The happy couple were astonished to hear more than one person say their betrothal did not surprise them. It seemed almost everyone at one time or another had remarked the couple only had eyes for one another and surely they would wed.

Lawrence pulled Meg from their enthusiastic crowd of well-wishers and brought her onto the center of the ballroom. The mass of people surrounding them backed away to give the notable couple room for their solo dance. The strings of a waltz began. Lawrence gallantly bowed. Meg made her curtsey and then he swept her into his arms not worrying about the twelve inch rule of separation that governed dancing partners. They made quite a matched pair dressed in their Elizabethan clothes, moving with grace across the parquet polished floors. Meg knew with the look in Lawrence's eyes, his confident hold of her body and his assured steps, the Reluctant Viscount was reluctant no longer. Her future was secure. Lawrence reveled in Meg's bright-eyed smile and grinned back at her. They each professed "I love you" at the same time and laughed to the amusement of their watchful audience.

Acknowledgements

I want to thank my readers for their helpful feedback, especially my editor, Alicia Floyd, who faithfully and diligently reviews my work, making recommendations and corrections. My body of work continually improves because of her queries, suggestions, and insight and I am forever grateful for her editing.

Thank you Christina Brusaca, my photographer, who manages to make my simple covers intriguing and to my son Lawrence, who posed for the book's cover.

My sincere appreciation to my friends and family, especially my husband Larry, my children, and parents, for their continued support and encouragement.

About the Author

Teresa Sweeney is a wife and mother of four adult children. She loves to read, write, and a myriad of other pursuits where she can use her creativity and imagination. She takes great pleasure penning historical romance novels that focus on the charm, wit, and banter of courtship. Visit her website www.teresa-sweeney.com for the latest information on her novels.

www.ingramcontent.com/pod-product-compliance
Lightning Source LLC
Chambersburg PA
CBHW030527310726
48979CB00010B/1828/J

* 9 7 8 1 9 4 0 3 1 9 0 3 2 *